Published by Pink Tree Publishing Limited in 2023

All characters and events in this publication, other than those clearly in the public domain, are fictitious and any resemblance to real persons, living or dead, is purely coincidental.

Copyright © Pink Tree Publishing Limited.

The moral right of the author has been asserted.

All rights reserved. This book or any portion thereof
may not be reproduced or used in any manner whatsoever
without the express written permission of the publisher
except for the use of brief quotations in a book review.

For questions and comments about this book, please contact
pinktreepublishing@gmail.com

www.pinktreepublishing.com
www.agathafrost.com

WANT TO BE KEPT UP TO DATE WITH AGATHA FROST RELEASES? *SIGN UP THE FREE NEWSLETTER!*

www.AgathaFrost.com

You can also follow **Agatha Frost** across social media. Search 'Agatha Frost' on:

Facebook
Twitter
Goodreads
Instagram

ALSO BY AGATHA FROST

Claire's Candles

1. Vanilla Bean Vengeance
2. Black Cherry Betrayal
3. Coconut Milk Casualty
4. Rose Petal Revenge
5. Fresh Linen Fraud
6. Toffee Apple Torment
7. Candy Cane Conspiracies

Peridale Cafe

1. Pancakes and Corpses
2. Lemonade and Lies
3. Doughnuts and Deception
4. Chocolate Cake and Chaos
5. Shortbread and Sorrow
6. Espresso and Evil
7. Macarons and Mayhem
8. Fruit Cake and Fear
9. Birthday Cake and Bodies
10. Gingerbread and Ghosts

11. Cupcakes and Casualties

12. Blueberry Muffins and Misfortune

13. Ice Cream and Incidents

14. Champagne and Catastrophes

15. Wedding Cake and Woes

16. Red Velvet and Revenge

17. Vegetables and Vengeance

18. Cheesecake and Confusion

19. Brownies and Bloodshed

20. Cocktails and Cowardice

21. Profiteroles and Poison

22. Scones and Scandal

23. Raspberry Lemonade and Ruin

24. Popcorn and Panic

25. Marshmallows and Memories

26. Carrot Cake and Concern

27. Banana Bread and Betrayal

Other

The Agatha Frost Winter Anthology

Peridale Cafe Book 1-10

Peridale Cafe Book 11-20

Claire's Candles Book 1-3

ABOUT THIS BOOK

Step back into the quaint village of Peridale, where café-owner, Julia South-Brown, finds herself entangled in a gripping new mystery. When the owner of the local food bank, Hilda, seeks her help after a break-in by a dear friend, Ronnie, Julia is drawn into a tangled web of secrets and deceit.

Determined to protect the community from scandal, Hilda entrusts Julia with the case, urging her to uncover the truth behind Ronnie's inexplicable actions. But as Julia volunteers at the food bank, the situation takes a sinister turn when Ronnie is murdered, just days after being hailed as the saviour of the struggling food bank in *The Peridale Post*.

With her daughter, Jessie, by her side, Julia delves deeper into Fern Moore's food bank, uncovering shocking revelations about Ronnie's past. A web of suspects emerges, including a jealous fellow volunteer, a resentful brother, an angry neighbour, a cunning businessman, and an old school acquaintance.

Elsewhere, Jessie faces several blasts from her past while making big decisions about her future, Julia's husband, Barker is working on his second book while lending his PI skills, and her sister, Sue, is settling into her new role working at the café. In a race against time, can Julia juggle family, business, and bringing justice to a close-knit community that has been rocked to the core before more volunteers suffer the same fate as Ronnie?

1

The scorching heat of the first week in July draped over Peridale like a suffocating blanket, eclipsing the season's cooler beginning. Nowhere felt it more than Julia's Café. Nestled across from the central green at the village's heart, it brimmed with its usual Saturday bustle.

Customers filled the seats, relishing iced drinks, while a few others still preferred hot beverages, contributing to the rich aroma of lingering coffee in the air. Menus danced in hands, emitting a whimsical warble that intertwined with the easy-listening pop songs on the radio. Atop the illuminated display case overflowing with cakes, the creaking fan proved useless against the near-tropical gusts ushered in by the ceaseless opening and closing of the front door.

Julia South-Brown helmed the counter, and after years of café experience, she took the buzz in her stride. She wore her usual welcoming smile while slicing and serving that morning's baking efforts. The carrot cake and lemon drizzle were almost gone, but she'd make more if the place quietened. Baking was her therapy, and her café was her sanctuary—even on the busiest Saturdays.

"And we haven't even hit the lunchtime rush yet," said Sue, her younger sister, pushing through the beaded curtain from the kitchen. She carried a tray loaded with sandwiches, a teapot, and scones stable on one arm, and chicken Caesar salads with a large jug of raspberry lemonade balanced on the other. Sue had recently swapped her blue nurse's scrubs for a pink apron, proving her ability to handle the chaos just as well in the café as she had on the wards. "Is it supposed to get any hotter today?"

"It is," offered Evelyn, who was reading the latest issue of *The Peridale Post* at the end of the counter. "Though I cherish these long summer days. Hard to believe there's a thunderstorm on the way next week."

Julia, busy at the till with a young customer ordering a long list of drinks, smiled at Evelyn. The local bed-and-breakfast owner had been brightening up the place in her buttercup yellow kaftan with a matching turban—similar in shade to the vibrant walls—all morning to keep the tables free. Julia always had time for her most regular customer, never one to shy away from proclaiming her predictions. "Did you see the storm in the tea leaves?"

Evelyn gave the paper a rustle. "It's in the forecast. I am enjoying the new weather section. Johnny Watson did a fine job as the editor, but Veronica has invigorated the pages since she took over. I was honoured she asked me to write the new horoscope section. Julia, you're a Virgo, aren't you?" She flipped back a few pages, her finger tracing the inky letters. "Here it is." She cleared her throat and announced, "'A new and intriguing challenge looms ahead. Your analytical and meticulous nature will serve you well. Tackle it with determination, trust your intuition, and depend on your discernment. Even if it seems daunting, trust in your capabilities, for the universe has chosen *you* for a reason.'"

"Can the universe delay the challenging call until this heatwave passes and the café calms down?" Julia asked, blowing a stray chocolatey curl that had slipped from her hair tie. "Push it to next year. I'd prefer things to stay exactly as they are right now."

"*Exactly* as they are?" Sue breezed behind the counter, joining Julia in preparing the takeaway drinks. "An extra pair of hands would be helpful today if the universe is listening. Do you think Jessie has finished her revision yet?"

Julia shrugged, reluctant to disrupt her daughter, who she hoped would have her face in a book in the flat above the post office next door.

"Jessie will do fine on her exam," Evelyn predicted. "Aquarius, Sue?"

"I'm not sure I believe in horoscopes, Evelyn."

"Found it," Evelyn continued, too lost reading her own predictions to hear Sue. "'You've taken a bold step towards a brighter future. The universe appreciates your courage. It's time to be satisfied with the decisions you've made.'"

Already in the rhythm of shaking up a cup of lemon iced tea, Sue raised an eyebrow. "Hmm. Accurate."

Evelyn tipped her turban in acknowledgement and continued reading, leaving the sisters to enjoy the café's pleasant chaos. The din of conversation echoed against the bright walls as the sun continued to shine outside, oblivious to Evelyn's impending thunderstorm prediction.

A little before noon, with no sign of things slowing down, a fresh gust of summer air brought in Dot, Julia and Sue's octogenarian grandmother. She wore her usual prim-and-proper outfit of a white blouse held at the collar with a brooch and tucked into a pleated navy skirt. She had the same issue of *The Peridale Post* that Evelyn had been reading. Dot wasted no time catching their attention with a wave. Julia shot her a questioning glance as her gran held up the paper's front page. The queue stretching to the door limited Julia's view. She glanced at Evelyn's copy, but she'd folded it inside out, leaving the sports page in view, now swirling the dregs in her teacup.

"Seems important," Sue said, as if reading her thoughts. "Emergency?"

Julia shook her head as Dot shuffled forward to let more customers tag on behind her. "She would've pushed to the front if it was."

"I foresee good news."

Julia and Sue exchanged glances at Evelyn's prediction, their lips pricking into the same knowing smile. Only the tapping of Dot's foot, inaudible over the crowd, hinted at her impatience.

After ten minutes of glaring at the backs of every customer who took their time reading the chalkboard menu, Dot reached the counter. She brandished the newspaper, lips primed in a purse.

"Tell that new neighbour of yours to get her facts straight," Dot said, her opening line no doubt the product of her wait. Never one to shy away from an audience in a packed café, Dot spoke low. "She couldn't have got Ronnie Roberts more wrong. He's a liar *and* a thief!"

Julia's heart skipped a beat as she read the headline, 'Local Hero Ronnie Roberts Saves Struggling Food Bank!' Disapproving frowns came from those who had overheard Dot's accusation.

"Pot of tea, Gran?" Julia dodged the claim about a man she didn't know, regretting not finding the time to read the latest issue to stay ahead. "I seldom see Veronica. The newspaper's only one of her jobs, and—"

"I can't stay. I had to come and show you this before walking the dogs with Percy. And she's likely too busy digging up false stories to print. She's painted a picture of Ronnie Roberts being a saint. After what Hilda Hayward told me over the telephone only half an hour ago, I might just set this new editor straight myself. Someone needs to recall these newspapers and edit them to include the truth about this so-called *hero*."

More disapproving looks pointed Dot's way, and this time she noticed and fired back her own challenging stares.

"Hilda runs the food bank in Fern Moore," Evelyn whispered, pointing to the outskirts of the village that many locals pretended didn't exist. "I'm always sending leftovers from the B&B her way. Lovely woman."

"She is," Dot agreed, stepping forward to lean against the counter. "I've been volunteering my time there. They've been struggling to get donations. That's one thing Veronica got right in her article, I suppose."

"Volunteering?" Sue said. "Not like you to keep your goings-on quiet."

"I started this week, but I don't need a neighbourhood watch group to do good in the community." She glanced at Evelyn and Julia, former members of the now-defunct Peridale's Ears group. She gave her grey curls a gentle push at the back, and said, "I've known Hilda since those food drives that we did around Christmas time. As Evelyn said, she is lovely, and she doesn't deserve what this Ronnie Roberts has done to her."

The two women next in line, growing more impatient, cleared their throats.

"I'll take two teas to go," Dot said, glancing over her shoulder at the queue spilling onto the pavement. Sue got to work making the drinks, but Dot leaned across the counter to Julia while she punched the order into the till, though she hit the 'Gratis' button. "Ronnie Roberts burgled Hilda's cottage last night. The man has some nerve, especially after everything Hilda has done for him. Once you're done with my teas and I've taken the dogs out, we'll get straight across to Fern Moore. You can hear the full story from Hilda."

"Gran, I'm a little busy right now. How am I involved in this?"

"I told Hilda you'd help her understand *why* Ronnie would want to break into her house," Dot said with a sigh, as though it should have been obvious. "The poor woman is distraught. Ronnie has desecrated her home, violated her trust, and nobody can solve a mystery like you, and I told her as much."

"As flattered as I am, I—"

"Hilda's adamant she doesn't want to go to the police," Dot charged on, eyelids fluttering, "which, for the record, I urged her to." She craned her slender neck at the beaded curtain. "Where's Jessie, anyway? Wasn't Sue hired so you could have more time away?"

"The café would still be busy, even if Jessie wasn't revising."

"Two teas *to go*." Sue placed the cardboard cups atop the newspaper, a supportive hand on Julia's shoulder. "Anything else, Gran? Not that we don't love your company, but we have other customers."

Dot's lips parted, and Julia expected her to put up a fight, but she peeped at the queue again, now reaching the picnickers on the green. She grabbed the cups with a strained smile and said, "You two are proving to make quite the café team. But mark my words, Julia. There's something peculiar about this man. If I can't convince Hilda to take this matter to the police, any of us could be next in line. Do you want a smashed kitchen window and a hooded figure lurking in the shadows after midnight? I promised Hilda you'd investigate things, so please think about it."

Knowing it would help move her gran along, Julia promised she would, and Dot left behind the paper. The picture underneath the headline showed a grizzled-looking man somewhere in his fifties grinning next to an older woman with a bubble of white hair. They stood in front of the metal shutters that Julia recognised as being somewhere over on the Fern Moore estate. The women with the matching perms stepped forward, so Julia tucked the newspaper under the counter.

"Would you look at the time?" Evelyn announced, her usual light tone coloured with uncharacteristic haste as she pulled away from the counter. "I'm late for checkouts."

"Evelyn, are you all right?" Julia asked.

"Yes, I'm sure it's nothing," Evelyn assured, her eyes darting down to the teacup before she scurried out of the café.

Sue picked up the abandoned teacup, her eyes

widening as she glanced inside. "When did you we start loose-leaf tea?"

"We don't," Julia replied. "She must've ripped open the tea bag."

"How do you interpret this?"

The sisters leaned in close, peering into the teacup where the leaves had settled.

Julia swallowed. "It looks like a skull."

"Evelyn got my horoscope spot on. Are you a believer?"

Despite Evelyn's belief in the supernatural, Julia shook her head and took the cup to the kitchen. She turned on the tap, rinsing away the mushy blob without hesitation. The tinkling bell above the door snapped her back to reality. She wasn't about to let mystics and madness derail her day. Not when she had a café full of customers to attend to. She dried her hands on her apron and stepped back into the lively hum, pushing her concerns aside for the moment.

This was her sanctuary, and Julia was needed.

2

By late afternoon, the café was still busy, making the hectic day feel like it had been a few intense hours long. After bidding farewell to the last customer, Father David Green from St. Peter's Church—who had spent the better part of the last hour regaling Julia with tales of his recent camping trip—Julia breathed a sigh of relief as Sue locked the door and flipped the sign.

"If every Saturday was like this, we could take the rest of the week off," Sue remarked, returning to the till to tally the day's earnings.

"For the sake of my aching feet, I hope the thunderstorm comes next weekend," Julia replied, massaging her arches after kicking off her burgundy

Oxfords and sinking into a chair near the counter. "How are you still standing?"

"You should try a Saturday in A&E. I have some fuel left. Though considering last weekend's eight-hour wait times I heard about from some nurses, avoid the place."

"I'll steer clear of any accidents or emergencies for the time being."

"That would be wise." Sue offered a laugh, tinged with a hint of sadness. "You know, I still…"

Sue started counting the money and her voice trailed off, but Julia understood her unspoken words. Six years her junior at thirty-six, Julia could read her sister like a book, and Sue still felt guilty about leaving the hospital.

Julia pushed herself back into her shoes and onto her feet. "Anything you want to talk about? I could go for a cup of peppermint and liquorice tea if you don't mind making one last drink."

"I do mind," Sue replied, her smile forced as she dropped the money into an empty envelope. "And I was right. Might be our best day of the summer so far. Go home and take a bath. I'll finish up here."

"Are you sure, I—"

"Hand over the apron and go home," Sue interrupted, flapping her hand for the apron. "Kiss your husband, hug your baby, and then slip into a bubble bath and don't get out until you're a prune. Nurse's orders."

"I'm not sure I can handle the extra heat right now."

"You realise your bath has a cold tap too?" Sue winked. "Now go. Neil's mum has the twins for the weekend, so we're having a date night. Katie's dropping by when she's finished at her salon to sort my nails out, and I brought my stuff to freshen up here so I can go straight across to Richie's." She gestured at the bar across the green before helping Julia out of her apron. She gave Julia a quick kiss on the cheek and a hug, adding, "I'd be working a double shift right now, dealing with broken bones, bleeding heads, and every bodily fluid you can imagine if you hadn't given me this job, so thank you."

"I should be the one thanking you. I don't know how we ever managed this place without you."

"That's just the exhaustion talking," Sue said, turning Julia toward the door and giving her a gentle push. "Even Superwoman gets tired feet after a long day, especially at your age."

"And you can consider this your first verbal warning."

Leaving the café with laughter, which had become a regular occurrence since Sue joined the team, Julia climbed into her beloved vintage Ford Anglia parked in the alley between the café and the post office. She reversed out and drove past Richie's towards the lane that would take her home, grateful she never had to doubt leaving the café in her sister's capable hands.

As she drove up the winding country lane to her small two-bedroom cottage, the last stop before Peridale Farm and the sprawling countryside, her anticipation for what awaited her was interrupted by the sight of her new neighbour, Veronica Hilt, who was mowing her lawn. Veronica always seemed to be in a rush, only ever having time to wave whenever they crossed paths.

Today, Veronica waved and stopped her sprint-mowing to approach the low stone wall surrounding her garden. Julia pulled alongside, cranking down her old car's stiff window. Veronica's dishevelled grey hair and mismatched bright clothes suggested she always got dressed in a hurry, too, though her oversized glasses distracted from the rest of her appearance.

"Evening, Julia," Veronica said, wiping her forehead with the side of her arm as the car groaned to a halt. "I tried to catch you earlier, but your café was packed, and I had a pile of marking to do for the college along with interviewing another of the sorry-excuses-for-journalists the higher-ups keep sending me." She sighed, suppressing a yawn. "Busy day?"

"The busiest," Julia replied, her interest piqued by

her neighbour's want of her. She had given little thought to Ronnie Roberts or her gran's allegations all afternoon, so it wriggled to the forefront of her mind without the refreshing list of orders rattling around in her head. "You were looking for me?"

Veronica leaned against the wall, and Julia braced herself for another question about whether she was going to investigate the break-in. "I was wondering if you could help me with something."

"Is this about Ronnie?"

Veronica's glasses magnified the surprise in her eyes. "No, it was about roses. I can't seem to keep them as beautiful as they were when I moved in, and the woman who sold me this place." She snapped her fingers together. "Leslie?"

"Leah," Julia corrected the name of her old school friend. "Leah Burns."

Veronica nodded, suppressing another yawn. "I promised Leah I wouldn't cut down her mother's roses, but I have no idea what to do with them. I feel like I'm disrespecting a deceased woman, and I don't have time to be haunted by a lady wielding pruning shears in the middle of the night."

"That would be Emily," Julia said, lowering her voice. "And don't worry, she moved away before she died, so I think you might be safe from any recent hauntings."

"I'll sleep easier tonight." Veronica laughed, squinting at Julia. "You thought I was going to ask about Ronnie? Ronnie Roberts, I assume?" She paused for Julia to nod. "Don't tell me you found an error in the paper. I had some mad old woman yelling at me about 'getting everything wrong' when I was trying to enjoy my lunch outside the pub earlier. The people here are quite interesting."

Julia joined in the laughter, hoping Veronica couldn't see how flushed her face had become. "Peridale has its characters. But yes, I meant Ronnie Roberts. I don't suppose you've heard anything about him breaking into someone's house?"

"Ronnie?" Veronica's eyebrows shot up in surprise, breaking the border of her glasses. "No? Whose house?"

"Hilda Haywards', apparently."

"No. He wouldn't. He seemed like a nice fella. Ex-army." Her gaze drifted off towards Fern Moore. "He joked about being a 'bad boy' in the past, but I didn't think much of it. From what I heard when I was writing my article, he's single-handedly keeping the food bank afloat. Are you sure we're talking about the same person?"

Julia considered asking more about the man, but Barker and Olivia were waiting by the gate, and Olivia had noticed the aqua blue car. If Julia had stolen a moment to herself all day, she might have read the newspaper. She'd left it under the counter, but it would all be online. "You know, I might have heard wrong. You know what gossip is like. Starts off as one thing, and before you know it, there's not a shred of truth left." She tried to brush it off with a chuckle, but Veronica's stern expression didn't change. "My gardening skills are limited to cutting grass and pulling weeds. I'm sorry I can't be of more help."

"I'm sure I'll figure it out," Veronica replied, her stare still stuck on Fern Moore. "How's your Jessie doing with her revision, anyway?"

A pang of guilt hit Julia. She had been so busy with the day that she hadn't checked in on Jessie, despite her having been just a stone's throw away. Jessie dropped into the café at least once on her days off, but she'd avoided the place like Veronica had when she saw the queue snaking out the door. She shared this with her neighbour, and after some small talk about the heat, Julia let her get back to her frenzied mowing. She parked a little further up the lane behind Barker's car, where Olivia was waiting to leap into her arms.

"Hi, Mummy," Olivia said, followed by babble. She held up a small stuffed rabbit clutched in her grip that looked like it had come from a Happy Meal. "Cat!"

"Rabbit, Olivia, but close enough," Barker corrected, kissing Julia on the cheek. "Good day?"

"Long day."

"You and me both." Veronica wasn't the only one holding back yawns. "Anything exciting happen?"

"I'm not sure yet." Julia glanced in Fern Moore's direction. She walked up the garden path with Olivia, relieved to be home. "I'll tell you later, but first, my dear husband, is that the sound of a running bath I hear?"

Jessie could feel her brain pulsing as she flipped to the next page of her biology textbook spread out in front of her on the antique writing desk. Pushed up to the front window in her small flat above the post office, it gave her a view over the green as the sun slipped away. The desk, with its intricate carvings, was a gift from Brian, Julia's dad, for her recent twenty-first birthday. It was supposed to inspire her 'exam success and all future endeavours.' She blinked up from the book, not sure if it was doing anything to help the words on the page sink in.

Homeostasis.

Enzymes.

Photosynthesis.

Why did she need to know any of this?

The day had slipped away without her noticing, and she still had a mountain to go over before her exam on Monday. But that's what she got for leaving the science revision for last-minute cramming.

"Last one," she muttered aloud. "I've got this."

Blinking down at a diagram of the structure of a cell, she knew there was no way she'd 'got this', at least not tonight. She slapped the book shut, pushed it away, and leaned back in the swivel chair she'd borrowed from Barker's office under the café. She'd nicked it a week ago, and he still hadn't noticed. It wasn't like he was going down there much since he started that new book about the time capsule body dug up at the school last year.

Jessie looked around the flat, her only company her ever-growing army of plants. She could have gone the rest of her life without knowing the intricate details of how plants turned sunlight into food, but it wasn't even like she could blame a school for forcing her to sit the exams. Jessie had avoided that the first time around, a fact she had grown to regret with each new exam since deciding to take her GCSEs at the local college, a decision made after one too many espresso martinis at Johnny and Leah's wedding before Christmas.

Scrolling through the few takeaways still open on

her phone, she didn't want to pick the chicken shop over near Fern Moore again. Her stomach still didn't feel right after those weird wings she'd eaten after her maths revision last week. Before she could pick from the five places still open, an unknown number flashed on the screen, and Jessie's immediate assumption was that it was yet another call centre trying to sell her something she didn't need. But this late at night? She almost ignored it, but there was always a possibility it could be her brother.

"Hello?" she said and waited in silence. "That you, Alfie?" Still, there was no answer. "If that's you, bro, I can't hear you if you're talking to me."

There was a sharp intake of breath and nothing more, as though someone had stopped themselves from saying what was on the tip of their tongue.

"Look, if this is a prank, you've picked the wrong—"

The unknown caller hung up, and Jessie was about to return the call when the buzzing of the front door made her drop the phone with a clunk onto the old wood. She added another dent to the surface, but it wasn't like it was the first. Brian had insisted the marks gave the desk character. Jessie was sure he'd given it to her instead of chucking it headfirst into a skip.

"Who's there?"

"Your favourite English tutor turned editor. Bad time?" the familiar voice of Veronica sang down the phone in a tone that didn't quite suit her. "Don't suppose you have a minute?"

Jessie exhaled, letting out the weird tension from the one-two punch of the phone call, followed by the buzzer. She needed to eat and go to bed.

"Revision going that bad?" Veronica asked, looking around the place. She hadn't been inside before, but she didn't make a comment. Jessie grabbed the pile of clothes off the sofa and dumped them with more clothes on the dining table. "Sorry if I'm disturbing—"

"No," Jessie said, smiling away her lack of politeness. "Sorry, long day. Don't suppose you tried to call me just now?"

Veronica shook her head, and Jessie offered her a seat, but she lingered by the stairs. "I know it's late. I was just out to grab a pint of milk, and I thought I'd drop by and see how you were getting on."

"You needed a pint of milk this late?"

"For the morning." She fiddled with her gigantic glasses, her frames a bright turquoise; she had a different colour every time Jessie saw her. "Okay, it is as obvious as it seems. Thought any more about my offer?"

Jessie let out another sigh, not knowing how many

times she could tell her tutor she wasn't ready to leave the café, wasn't ready to dive headfirst into the world of journalism, wasn't ready to...

"Look, I know you think you're not ready," Veronica said in a whisper, taking a step further. "I get it. You don't want to rock the boat, don't want to take the leap. It's fair, Jessie. You're settled, but I will not stop asking until you seem *certain* this isn't something you want to give a go. I see real potential in you. If you can master analysing Shakespeare, you can write for the local paper."

Jessie glanced at the thick file that Johnny Watson, the previous editor of the paper, had thrust upon her before he left the village that spring. A file stuffed with information about Greg Morgan, their local Member of Parliament. Schedules, accounts, emails, and Jessie still hadn't been able to make any more sense of it than she could about the biology revision.

Veronica moved into the cottage across from her mum's that same night. The same night she'd offered Jessie a job at the newspaper she'd taken the reins of. The same night Jessie had declined. And again, a week later, and again at her twenty-first birthday party at Richie's in May, and twice more in June, and now...

"I won't ask again," Veronica said, taking a step back as she pulled out a lanyard with a plastic card attached. She draped it over the end of the banister. "I see the latest issue of the paper on your coffee table, so if you've read it, you already know half of the story. The man on the front cover broke into someone's home, and I've already interviewed him once in a very different context. I wouldn't ask, but I need someone undercover to ask around, and I still have a pile of marking to get through before Monday. If Mr Roberts isn't all he seems, the people have a right to know after I gave him such a ringing endorsement."

"I read it," Jessie confirmed, leaving out that she already knew Ronnie. "I'm not sure what you want me—"

"There's a fundraiser at Fern Moore tomorrow around lunchtime and there's a high chance he'll be there. I need a couple of quotes to see what he has to say for himself. Maybe ask around about him. It shouldn't take long."

Jessie looked at her desk. It wasn't like she'd planned to spend all of Sunday revising. More than anything, she'd wanted to give her brain a break for at least some of the day, maybe tag along with Dot and Percy on one of their dog walks, but somehow, she felt like she owed Veronica.

"A couple of quotes?"

"A couple of quotes."

If Veronica hadn't pushed her so hard, her English coursework would never have gone from a C to an A.

"Fine," Jessie agreed with a conceding sigh. "A couple of quotes."

Veronica didn't linger, likely not wanting Jessie to change her mind.

Alone again, slumping back in the chair, Jessie moved the ID around in her hands and let the desk lamp catch the holographic foil. A year-younger version of her grinned from a blurry square, a selfie taken during her globetrotting. Those days already seemed so long ago, and she'd been home for almost a year. It was the same ID Johnny had given her when she'd helped with the allotment case.

Journalism had never been in her plan.

But neither was working in a café, nor taking on her exams five years after she was supposed to. She'd been too busy being homeless back then. Homeless with men like Ronnie Roberts. The 'ringing endorsement' hadn't convinced her when she'd read it either, so it didn't surprise her to hear he'd gone back to his old ways.

The ID went onto the Greg Morgan folder, replacing it with her phone, and Jessie considered calling the unknown number back. A wrong number and she was too tired to care, yet too hungry to sleep. Back in the takeaway app, the five options she'd had to pick from before Veronica had interrupted had whittled down to the one chicken shop near Fern Moore.

Immersed in a soothing soup of Epsom salts and lavender essential oils, encased under a layer of foamy bubbles, Julia contemplated two things. First, she marvelled at her incredible luck at having a husband like Barker. Second, she couldn't help but wonder how she had spent the entire day without giving much thought to the break-in. If the café had been abuzz with gossip, she'd have had no choice. On such busy days, it was difficult to filter out anything amidst the noise, and what she had caught, in typical Peridale fashion, revolved around the weather.

The 'mad old woman' who had disrupted Veronica's lunch at The Plough had to be Julia's gran. It would only be a matter of time before the gossip spread through the village like wildfire. In her rush, Julia had dismissed Dot. It wouldn't be the first time her gran had hurried to share gossip that Julia couldn't make sense of. But the more Julia pondered the conflicting sides of the smiling man on the front page, the more concerned she became, especially now that she knew about the food bank hero's army background. Fingers would point at her grandmother as the source of misinformation if she had things wrong, as Julia hoped.

But Veronica's comment about Ronnie admitting to being a 'bad boy' had caught Julia's attention. She glanced at her clothes hanging on the back door and spotted her phone nestled in the pocket of that day's vintage lilac summer dress. She considered climbing out to read the article, only to sink deeper into the steam.

The article could wait.

The bath couldn't.

Despite her uncertainty about handling the heat after a clammy day, the nurse's orders had been well-prescribed, making her all the gladder to have her sister by her side in the café. Sue had brought some much-needed balance to the place, relieving Julia of a few of the many responsibilities she juggled in her life. She'd meant it when she'd told Evelyn that she wanted things to remain as they were.

Sue was spending more time with her twins, and Julia could spend more time at home with Olivia. Barker's private investigator business had taken a backseat while he worked on his long-awaited second novel at home, allowing them to retreat into the home life bubble they had created during the early days of parenthood when the world had seemed to stand still around them. Not being scheduled until Wednesday made her sink lower in the bath.

With the salts and steam working their magic on her muscles, and the candles and music soothing her mind, Julia allowed her heavy eyelids to close. She wondered if she could avoid delving deeper into what her grandmother had shared with her.

All at once, Julia jolted awake, her skin prickling from the sudden coldness in the water. The playlist was now silent, the calming chimes replaced by the startling sound of Olivia coming from the nursery next door. Olivia's cries took on a sharp, panicked note that sent Julia's heart into overdrive. Pruned fingertips caught the tiles as she slipped on the settled oils and salt.

"Teething," she muttered to herself, wrapping a towel around her before racing from the bathroom. The wail from the nursery intensified, sending a shiver down her spine. She dashed down the hallway, her heart pounding as Mowgli, their smoky grey Maine Coon, raced past in the opposite direction.

Olivia was standing in her cot, the celestial nightlight stretching her shadow up to the cottage's beamed ceiling. Her tiny hands gripped the rails, her soft cheeks flushed scarlet and streaked with tears. Unless Olivia was growing all four wisdom teeth at once before her baby set had finished poking through, her cries weren't something a teething ring from the freezer could fix.

"Shh, it's okay."

Julia lifted Olivia out, feeling her daughter's tiny hands trembling with each sob. She checked under the cot and peeked in the wardrobe, but Olivia's fearful gaze was fixed on the window, and as Julia turned to follow her daughter's line of sight, her breath froze. The blind was thick enough to block out the last of the setting sun, but the shifting light bled around the edges in a perfect square. Clutching Olivia close, she felt her tiny heart beating against her own.

"Is someone there?" Julia's voice echoed in the quiet nursery.

In response to her demand, a shadow outside the window retreated, and a soft voice filtered in through the blind. "I saw the light on and thought someone was in here. I knocked on the front door first."

Julia yanked up the blind, and her gaze met with an elderly woman standing in the garden under the fading light of dusk. The stranger's hair glowed a pale silver, arranged in a halo around her open face. A pair of spectacles perched on her nose, their lenses reflecting the nursery's soft glow. An apologetic smile curled her lips upwards, etching lines of remorse on her face as she registered Olivia's continued distress.

Barker burst into the room, headphones around

his neck and a waft of smoky air from the fire pit accompanying him. Papers rustled in his hands as he panted, his wide-eyed gaze flitting between Julia, sobbing Olivia, and the woman outside. "What's going on?"

Steadying her rattled nerves with a deep breath, Julia recalled seeing the woman earlier that day on the front page. "Hilda, isn't it? Hilda Hayward?"

The elderly woman looked relieved, her nod affirming Julia's guess. Barker took Olivia, her cries quieting into whimpers. While Barker was comforting Olivia, Julia left the nursery and ushered Hilda in through the front door. Hilda stepped into the cottage in a threadbare cardigan over a floral-print dress, resembling a grandmother pulled straight from the pages of a children's storybook, despite Olivia's reaction to her.

"I'm ever so sorry to have caused such a commotion," Hilda said, her voice fluttering like a soft breeze. "I should go. It's just...Dot suggested you might help with a problem I'm having."

Julia adjusted her slipping towel and managed a reassuring smile. "Stay, please. Do you like marshmallows, Hilda?"

Hilda hesitated before providing a shy nod. The shock from Julia's unexpected visitor was receding, and silence once again descended upon the cottage.

After pulling on her pink dressing gown and with Barker resettling Olivia for the night, Julia joined her unexpected guest by the fire pit at the bottom of the garden. She had already settled herself on the log and skewered two large marshmallows onto the ends of sticks.

"Again, I'm—"

"Apology accepted," Julia interjected, accepting a stick. "Did my gran give you my address?"

Hilda shook her head. "A young chap in the café over on the Fern Moore estate knew where you lived. Your gran said you'd pop by, and when you didn't, I suppose I felt a little desperate and started asking around. I don't know what else to do, Julia. Did your gran tell you what happened?"

"Ronnie broke into your house?"

Hilda nodded, her face trembling as if to hold back tears. So much for hoping Dot had the wrong end of the stick. With her marshmallow roasting over the fire, Hilda watched as the pink coating caramelised brown and didn't flinch as it darkened to a charcoal black. Sensing the story would not reveal itself, Julia pulled the stick away and set it on the grass, turning her attention to Hilda.

"I'm not promising I can help," Julia began, "but why don't you start from the beginning? My gran mentioned he smashed your kitchen window and—"

"There was a key under my doormat," Hilda corrected. "I left my keys at bingo once and put a spare there after walking to and from the bingo hall twice in one night. Never needed it, but I thought I'd be saving my legs. It's my fault."

"If someone breaks into your house, it's not your fault," Julia assured her, locking with Hilda's uncertain eyes as she glanced up. "I take it Ronnie is your friend?"

Hilda nodded and the tears she'd been fighting spilled down her crinkled cheeks. "A dear, dear friend. We met at the food bank. He'd bring donations of what he could spare every week without fail, and he always made time to chat and ask how I was. After my husband, Jack, died two years ago, he was there for me when no one else was. I thought I was doing a fine job hiding how much I was struggling with my grief. Fifty years of happy marriage does that. Keep calm and carry on, as they say," she paused, thumbing a wedding band on her left hand, and continued, "Ronnie noticed. He became a shoulder to cry on. A confidant. Ronnie was a soldier in the army, you see, and dreadful things tormented him. Things he should never have had to experience. I didn't know him until a few years ago, but he was the first to admit those things changed him, and despite his best intentions, he landed himself in some trouble."

Hilda paused, looking back at the flickering flames. Julia glanced at the cottage and noticed Barker observing from the kitchen window. He gave her a thumbs up as though checking in, and she nodded in response before turning back to Hilda.

"Trouble with the police?" Julia asked. "Is that why you don't want to report it?"

"I *will not* do that to him. The man has suffered enough. He turned his life around, you see. Ronnie has the gift of the gab. The people in the community like him. He's been instrumental in drumming up support for the food bank. Without him, we would have had to shut down months ago. I've been running the place for a decade now, but demand has long exceeded supply and it's only getting worse. Ronnie has helped to keep the community fed. He's not a wicked man."

"I think it's noble that you want to defend him, and it sounds like he's done a lot of good," Julia said, unable not to sigh, "but he broke into your house. Did he take anything?"

"I'm still trying to figure that out."

"Money? Valuables?"

"All present, but he turned the place upside down."

"Like he was searching for something?"

Hilda nodded.

"And there was no inkling beforehand?"

"None," Hilda said. "I didn't want to believe it could have been Ronnie when I returned from my weekly shopping trip yesterday afternoon and saw the state of my cottage. My neighbours saw him, you see, and it wasn't until they showed me the footage they captured on their cameras that I accepted it. If I hadn't picked such an obvious hiding spot..." More tears flowed, and Julia wished she had her handbag with her stash of handkerchiefs in hand. "Twenty minutes later, he ran out and hopped over the fence. I was ready to confront him at the fundraising meeting that evening, but I just couldn't bring myself to do it."

"You've seen him since?" The shock in Julia's voice was impossible to hide.

"We meet every Friday evening. Ronnie's been organising fundraisers every Sunday to drum up support. It's the day we give out the most food parcels. But on Friday, he just wasn't himself. I don't think he knows I know it was him, but he couldn't bring himself to look me in the eye. I haven't seen him at all today. When I rang your grandmother this morning to ask if she'd be joining us for the fundraiser, she picked up on something in my voice, and Dorothy seems like the sort of woman who doesn't mince her words, so it all came spilling out. When she said her granddaughter was an amateur detective, I felt a glimmer of hope that I might put this to rest."

"I'm more of a baker than a detective," Julia admitted, never at ease with her local reputation as a sleuth, though it wasn't inaccurate. "My husband's a private investigator. He might—"

"No officials. Your grandmother said you've solved more murders than the local police in recent years," Hilda urged, nodding as though she couldn't bear to leave without a commitment. She reached out and clasped both of Julia's hands in her own clammy grip. "Please, Julia, I don't know what else to do. Say you'll come to the fundraiser tomorrow. Ronnie will be there. He might talk to someone else. An impartial third party. I just want to know why he'd betray my trust like this. There must be an explanation."

Julia's vision of a quiet Sunday pottering around at home with Barker and Olivia vanished in an instant, her mind made up for her. How could she turn down that plea?

"I can't promise I'll be able to get to the bottom of things, but—"

"You'll come?" Hilda let her body's tension drop and glanced up at the sky, now peppered with stars. "Thank you, thank you, thank you. You don't know what this means to me."

"I think I do," Julia said, accepting Hilda's hug.

"But please, don't get your hopes up. I'll try to talk to Ronnie, but if he doesn't want to talk to me, you might not have any choice but to go to the police."

Hilda sprung up with more energy than she'd shown since appearing at Olivia's window. "I promise, I will. I'll need to set off or I'm going to miss the last bus back home. We open at noon, and again, I'm so sorry for startling your little one. And Julia, promise you'll keep this between us? Only you and your gran know so far. This can't spread. Regardless of what Ronnie's done, he doesn't deserve the whispering behind his back."

"You have my word."

"Then I'll leave you to enjoy the rest of your evening," Hilda said, embracing Julia in another quick hug. "Tomorrow at noon?"

"Tomorrow at noon."

As she watched Hilda hurry around the side of the cottage, Julia let out a groan as Barker set off down the garden path to join her with a steaming mug; she'd already broken her word by letting the news slip to Veronica Hilt, of all people.

"Would this be about Ronnie Roberts, by any chance?" Barker asked, handing over a cup of peppermint and liquorice tea while taking Hilda's place. "Your gran and Percy passed with the dogs earlier, and Dot told me all about some smash-and-grab burglary. I'm pretty sure she was trying to get me to agree to twist your arm to investigate."

Julia rested her head on his broad shoulder as she stared into her favourite minty sweet tea, still too hot to sip. "Consider my arm twisted. How's the book coming along?"

"Sticky middle. I need a break from the laptop."

"Then I might already have plans for us for tomorrow. How does a food bank fundraiser at Fern Moore sound?"

Hilda was indeed lovely, as Evelyn and Dot had said. Unravelling the why rather than the who, Julia would try her best to help. Not as an amateur detective, but as a friend to a woman who cared about her community as much as Julia did.

But first, Julia had to put a lid on the break-in before the story broke out of the frying pan and into the fire of *The Peridale Post*'s next front page.

3

*E*ven on a sunny afternoon, the utilitarian blocks of Fern Moore stood as an isolated island just outside the boundaries of the village, asserting their separateness. Given their snooping reasons for being there, Julia didn't put up a fight when Barker insisted they take his car instead of her 'old banger' the next morning. She didn't want her bright car, which still ran fine, to draw too much attention.

"So, the plan," Barker stated as he unloaded the pram after their donations box, while Julia adjusted Olivia's hat. "We find Ronnie Roberts, see if he's willing to talk, and then we get back home for our scheduled lazy Sunday?"

"Sounds like the perfect plan to me."

"The perfect plan would also include grabbing some fish and chips to eat with a couple of episodes of *Grand Designs*. The quicker we leave, the better. You know my opinion of this place."

Fern Moore's troubled reputation had preceded it throughout Julia's life, a place she would have once avoided like the plague. Barker had spent his fair share of time there chasing criminals during his brief tenure as the village's Detective Inspector when he first moved to the area. Most people from the estate were decent, despite a few bad apples, and it wasn't like Peridale didn't have its fair share of bad eggs too. But the reputation wasn't baseless, Julia knew that all too well. She'd had her pearl engagement ring, once belonging to her mother, snatched from her at the bus stop. If it hadn't been for Jessie tracking it down, it would never have made its way back to her hand. Somehow, Peridale's reputation, for all its faults, still aligned with the picturesque postcards that attracted the trickle of tourists every summer.

Today, it seemed like the tourists had spilt over into Fern Moore. At least, that's what Julia assumed from the nicer-than-usual clothes she saw. Tracksuit-wearing teenagers were still hanging out, drinking and vaping outside the few shops. However, there were more young professionals present, and the place had undergone another mini facelift since her last visit.

They noticed a long line snaking around one block, leading to a storage unit hidden down a tunnelled path. Julia glanced into her box of canned and jarred provisions collected from the café's pantry that morning. She noticed others in the queue were empty-handed, with those carrying boxes walking straight to the front. Julia smiled at those in need of the food bank's services as she passed with her donations.

"Sell your home for *instant* cash!" a man with a sweat-glistening face in a choking green tie barked, dropping a leaflet into Julia's box. "Competitive rates *guaranteed!*"

The man delivered the same speech to Barker, who stayed outside with Olivia. Inside the storage unit, with mottled concrete walls and faint dampness in the air, Julia found Hilda behind the counter, along with two unfamiliar women. Three women she recognised were plucking boxes of cereal and cans off the shelves: her gran, Shilpa from the post office, and Amy, the church organist.

Hilda's face lit up when she picked Julia out from the crowd. "You came! And you brought donations."

"I *told* you she'd come," Dot called with a wag of

her finger. "Whenever there's justice to be served, my granddaughter is never far behind."

Leaving the two unfamiliar women to man the counter, Hilda ushered Julia and her box to the shelves at the back, while Dot and the others huddled in.

"It's almost like the old Peridale Ears gang is back together," Dot said with a grin, pulling Shilpa and Amy in. "Isn't this fun?"

"We're not here for fun, Dorothy," Shilpa replied. "And I did only come to drop off the almost out-of-date stock from the post office."

"And I always bring the donations from the church every Sunday after service," Amy said, pulling away from Dot's tight grip and brushing down her pale pink cardigan. "Not that I don't mind offering my time, but I'm playing the organ at a wedding in a couple of hours, and—"

"But this is a *classic* Peridale's Ears case," Dot whispered, huddling them in further. "A mysterious break-in, a missing suspect, a—"

"Missing suspect?" Julia spoke up, sliding her heavy box onto a shelf. "Ronnie hasn't shown up?"

Hilda shook her head. "And nobody saw him yesterday. He's never missed a Sunday since he started volunteering. Georgiana and Audrey haven't seen him either." She gestured to the two women at the counter.

Julia wasn't sure who was who, but the younger one, with a snatched-back blonde ponytail, was doing a terrible impression of someone not eavesdropping, while the older of the two, with deep purple cropped hair, kept the parcels flying out. "Something must have happened. I fear he's in trouble again, and—"

"It's not like we need him," the woman with the ponytail said, her accent more refined than the local dialect. "In fact, today proves that we don't need Ronnie. Donations are still coming in."

Hilda sighed and pinched the bridge of her nose. "Yes, thank you, Georgiana."

"He's not the only one putting in the hard work here," Georgiana continued, her arms folding and her ponytail bobbing with each word. Julia would have guessed she was teetering on thirty. "I told you he'd be trouble, and him breaking into your house proves that."

"Will you keep your voice down?" Hilda hissed, wincing. "It's supposed to be a secret."

Julia gulped and wondered if her regretful slip of the tongue to Veronica was behind it. The story hadn't reached the digital pages of the newspaper yet, which was a relief. If Johnny had still been the editor, she could have twisted her old school friend's ear until he promised not to print the story, but she didn't so much as have Veronica's phone number.

"I'm unsure how much I can do without Ronnie," Julia said.

"He lives nearby," Hilda said, looping her arm through Julia's. "If he's in trouble, the least I can do is help."

Georgiana muttered something as they passed, and Julia wanted to tell Hilda she was the victim, but didn't bother. Barker shot her a quizzical look as Hilda rushed her past, and Julia could only shrug as she hurried to keep up.

"He's on the second floor, right in the middle," Hilda explained, releasing her grip as she hurried up the stairwell. "Lifts still break down bi-weekly despite the spending around here."

Despite her age, Hilda moved with haste, forcing Julia to take the steps two at a time to catch up. When she did, Hilda was knocking on the door of one flat where the TV blared.

"You telling him to turn that racket down?" a woman with long cherry-red hair demanded from the neighbouring window. Behind her, a toddler ran around. "Day and night, he never turns down the TV volume, but this is something else! Usually, he turns it off, but last night? None of us got a wink of sleep! I banged on the wall, but typical Ronnie ignored me, only caring about himself. I've half a mind to call the police so the pigs can sort him out."

"Yes, all right, Paige," Hilda replied in a similar tone to the one she had used with Georgiana. "You know Ronnie is a little hard of hearing."

"Yeah, and I will be too if he doesn't turn that thing off!" Paige slammed her window shut.

"They've had a few run-ins," Hilda explained in a whisper, knocking louder on the door. "Ronnie, are you in there? It's Hilda, Ronnie. I just want to talk."

The two of them waited while an old episode of *Dad's Army* played, a programme often on her gran's TV when Julia was growing up. Hilda continued knocking, but nobody answered.

"Maybe he's not in?" Julia suggested, glancing over the walkway at Barker, who had taken Olivia to the swings. "Did you figure out what he took from your home?"

"I didn't, and Ronnie is very conscious about his electricity meter. He'd never go out leaving the telly on, you see. I can't believe I'm about to suggest this, but I wonder if there's a spare key around here. I can't say I'm not worried right now."

Julia nodded down at the bristly doormat, and after surveying the otherwise empty walkway, Hilda reached down and pulled it back, revealing a rusted silver key. "Maybe leaving mine there wasn't so stupid. It's Hilda, Ronnie. Now's your chance to come to the door, or I'm coming in."

Hilda turned the key, and as the door swung open, a pungent smell hit Julia. It was a smell she wished she didn't recognise—a smell that nobody should know, but she did. The women exchanged fraught glances before stepping into the flat where the curtains were drawn, the only light flickering from the small flatscreen blaring the old army sitcom. The flickering images accentuated the outline of a man with a prominent bald spot slumped in the room's single armchair, pointed at the screen.

"R-Ronnie?" Hilda choked, her hand reaching out before covering her mouth, tears welling up in her eyes. "Oh, Ronnie."

4

Silence fell across Fern Moore when paramedics announced Ronnie Roberts, fifty-two, dead at the scene. The chatter ceased, the courtyard filled up with people watching on as officials turned up in their droves, and even the never-ceasing music retreated into the background.

Barker had taken Olivia home, shielding her from the grim reality that had unfolded. Back at the food bank, the queue was still going strong, leaving Hilda teetering on the edge of an obvious breakdown, her hands trembling as they moved about her tasks. Julia attempted to make her sit down, but she seemed entranced while handling parcels and accepting donations.

Georgiana, who had been outspoken earlier, had

now adopted an unsettling silence, while Audrey worked double-time, juggling her duties and Hilda's as well. Amy and Shilpa had left, leaving only Dot and Julia from the village. It was Dot, with a comforting hand on Hilda's shoulder, who coaxed the committed volunteer away from her tasks and into a chair, her protests faint whispers, her body not her own.

"We're closing up for today," Audrey announced, the decision prompting protesting moans.

Georgiana shrugged. "It's not the end of the world. Ronnie was a *part* of the food bank, not the *whole* thing." Her words hung in the air, her apathy a sour note. "Something like this was bound to happen. He was probably hitting the bottle again."

Dot voiced what Julia had suspected. "You never did like Ronnie, did you, Georgiana? I saw you sneaking off for a make-up touch-up while everyone else was crying."

Georgiana scoffed. "And what about it? Ronnie was no spring chicken. Old people die all the time."

"Spoken like an idiot in her twenties," Dot muttered, shaking her head.

"Ronnie was fit," Hilda countered, her voice quivering above the whispers she'd only been able to manage since the shock set in. "Ronnie stopped drinking years ago. He was close to death, but he recovered. He told me so. He never wanted to—"

"And I *always* said you couldn't believe a man like him," Georgiana continued, emboldened by the conflict. "He was a criminal that you never should have let in here, but you *needed* a poster child for the paper."

"That's enough." Audrey cut in, holding up a hand to Georgiana. "Dot's right. You sound like a foolish idiot right now. Ronnie could have died from anything. People can have hidden health issues even they don't know about. Ronnie wasn't drinking again, as far as I could tell."

"I don't understand any of this," Hilda said. "The break-in, his death, it makes so little sense. Why now? Audrey, you knew him from school, didn't you? Ronnie betraying me like that, was it in his character?"

Audrey shifted her weight from foot to foot, crossing her arms. "That was a long time ago, Hilda. I didn't really know him, and are any of us the same people we were as teenagers?"

"We *can* keep the food bank going without him," Georgiana piped up, her tone far too ambitious for the sombre air. "I've always said *I* have plenty of ideas for this place."

"Georgiana, this *isn't* the time," Audrey snapped. "Nobody wants to hear *your* ideas right now."

Georgiana stormed off after spinning around and

stomping her foot like a scolded child. On her way out, she almost banged into a greengrocer carrying crates of fruit and vegetables. He retreated after leaving the donations.

"These bananas are almost black!" Dot riffled through the contents. "And the potatoes are sprouting. What are we supposed to do with these? Give it a week or two and the potatoes my Percy has been growing at the allotment will be far superior."

"We take donations as they come," Audrey stated, already heaving the boxes to their relevant shelves. "Now, I'm locking up. For now, I think this is the last place any of us should be. Can I drive you home, Hilda?"

Hilda nodded. "Someone will need to tell Ronnie's brother. I know they weren't close, but…"

Hilda choked on her words, her pleading teary eyes fixed on Julia, but no other request followed. She longed to help the woman she had met for the first time yesterday, despite not knowing her well. She just wasn't sure how.

"I think we wait and see what the police say," Julia advised. Then, spotting the bananas low on the fruit shelf, she added, "As for these, I know what to do. If you don't mind me taking them, I promise I'll have something you can give out tomorrow."

Hilda nodded as she shuffled off, and with Audrey waiting to drag the metal shutter down, Dot and Julia decided it was time to return home. Each carrying a handle of the banana crate, they crossed the courtyard and Julia stared up at the walkway. Detective Inspector Laura Moyes from the neighbouring village of Riverswick nodded down at Julia with a curious squint.

"I *told* you there was something strange going on," Dot said, though she sounded more grave than triumphant. "Give your Barker a call to pick us up. I don't fancy walking home carrying enough bananas to feed a small monkey zoo."

"You *also* told me he smashed her kitchen window and was lurking about her house at midnight. He used a key under her doormat in the afternoon. Not the snatch-and-grab of the century, like you made out. And we can catch the bus."

"Hmm. Well, we better hurry. From those clouds, rain is on the way."

The sight of the dark clouds on the horizon recalled Evelyn's warning of a thunderstorm, along with the tea leaves she'd left behind in the shape of a skull. The unease Julia had felt peering into the cup returned. She wished she didn't now have a face to go with the skull. Glancing back at DI Moyes before they rounded the corner, Julia hoped Laura Moyes' presence there was routine and not the start of another murder case.

∽

Parking her car in the only available space outside of McSizzle's, Jessie regretted indulging in the late-night takeaway. The chicken wrap with extra mayo had left her feeling fine, but the hour-long wait for the delivery and subsequent hours of digestive tossing and turning before falling asleep had taken its toll. Yawning, she glanced at her phone. So, not quite noon, but it wasn't like she'd promised to be on time.

A couple of quotes about Ronnie Roberts.

Easy.

They used to call him 'Rotten Ronnie' back when the Fenton Industrial Park served as a makeshift village for the homeless. Ronnie never resorted to begging on the streets like the others, but he had a knack for nicking. If you were lucky enough to have a few beer cans to keep you warm at night or some extra coins, you had to hold them close around Ronnie. Jessie had only needed to land a single punch on his jaw once to get him to leave her alone.

They'd long since swept everyone away and redeveloped the area back to its original purpose, and

Jessie hadn't needed to use her fists in a while, but the memories of those days would forever linger.

With her head down, Jessie hurried past a scattering of police officers and darted around an ambulance. The estate was always buzzing, so she was grateful for the village's one day of Sunday stillness. But the estate was quieter than usual despite appearing busy.

As she reached the wooden climbing frames in the middle, her steps slowed to a halt. A black body bag was being carried down the stairwell. Beside her, a man removed his flat cap and cracked open a can of beer. He poured a fizzling splash on the concrete, his actions accompanied by a restrained sniffle, and he wasn't the only one crying.

"See you on the other side, Ronnie," he said, taking a slurp. "You were one of the good ones."

Jessie's jaw dropped as she watched the body bag being loaded into the back of a coroner's van. She was struggling to process the situation, her mind racing.

"Excuse me," she whispered to the man. "Is that Ronnie Roberts?"

He nodded, rubbing away a tear from his cheek.

Miss an hour.

Miss a lot.

Jessie wiped away a surprising tear of her own. Thoughts of Fenton Industrial Park had crossed her mind often since she found a family in Peridale, and she had always wished the best for everyone she'd left behind, even if she never trusted Ronnie. She'd been filled with guilt in the early days—the one that got away. Ronnie died with a roof over his head, but it wasn't much consolation.

"Sorry, but do you know what happened?" she croaked.

"Died watching telly."

Before the man could elaborate further, a brewing commotion across the courtyard diverted attention away from the coroner's van. Outside Daphne's Café, a group of lads dressed in black tracksuits were shoving someone around as if they were in a school corridor with no teachers present. Uniformed police officers rushed at them from all directions.

"Have you no *shame*?" one lad yelled, landing a sloppy punch in the victim's gut. "A man has just died!"

The group parted, allowing Jessie to glimpse a man in a tailored suit with a green tie, collecting himself as the police pulled the aggressors away. People shook their heads in his direction as he scrambled to gather leaflets scattered on the concrete.

Out of nowhere, a lad on an electric scooter, concealed by a balaclava, zoomed past, snatching the leaflets from the man, and delivering a swift kick to his groin. The crowd erupted in a mix of shock and amusement, their cheers merging with the sound of the scooter's motor. People made way, creating a path for the mysterious figure to make a hasty escape. The officers, already on high alert, gave chase.

She watched as the vigilante sped towards the corner where the CostSavers mini supermarket stood. The scooter's wheels skidded as it attempted to make a sharp turn. In an instant, the rider lost control and vanished beneath the crowd.

Despite disapproving jeers from the onlookers, no one dared to challenge the officers as they swooped in. He was subdued despite the sounds of a scuffle and grunts of protest. With a firm grip, they dragged him through the crowd, who'd taken to booing, the body bag already a distant memory. As they reached the nearest parked police car, one officer dragged down the balaclava, revealing the reddened face beneath.

Jessie's breath caught in her throat.

"B-Billy?"

Time seemed to stand still as her gaze locked with the scooter driver, forgetting the unfolding chaos. The last years of her teens flickered through her mind like a film playing on fast-forward. Billy Matthews' mischievous grin and piercing blue eyes were unmistakable, even after two years.

Before Jessie could gather her thoughts, they

forced Billy into the back of a police car, unable to take his eyes off Jessie. The door slammed shut, leaving Jessie bewildered as the crowd dispersed. Somewhere in the distance, music cranked up, its stuttering drumbeats jolting her back to reality, reminding her of why she was even on the estate. The car sped off, those blue eyes watching her until they rounded the corner.

But the urgency left with the coroner's van.

Ronnie was dead.

And Billy, her ex-boyfriend, was back.

5

*J*ulia treasured her mother's handwritten recipe book, lovingly worn and stained from years of use. Whenever she had the chance, she would pull it out and relish the memories of her childhood. This rainy summer night was no different, even with death on her mind. Her intention was to write a shopping list for the ingredients needed to make a bulk load of banana bread using the overripe bananas that waited on the counter. However, the allure of the recipe book faded as her mind fixated on the two words she had written: Ronnie Roberts.

Julia's thoughts were about to be consumed by the mystery surrounding Ronnie's death when Hilda hurried into the kitchen, let in by Barker. Julia welcomed the distraction.

"I can't stay long," Hilda said, her voice tinged with weariness. Her purple eyes betrayed signs of the tears shed earlier. "Audrey's waiting outside, and I think she's eager to get home. She's been looking after me at my cottage all day."

"I'm glad you had someone with you," Julia replied. "The two of you seem close."

"We're the two surviving founding members of the food bank," she said, looking around the kitchen as though she'd paid it no attention the first time. "Listen, I want to apologise for getting you involved. I never imagined it would escalate like this, but here we are. Ronnie's dead, and the police are calling it murder."

Julia had already heard the official news from Roxy, another old school friend and DI Moyes' girlfriend, but she kept that information to herself, sensing there was more Hilda wanted to share.

"They're saying he was poisoned," she whispered. "I don't know what to make of this, but they think it happened on Friday night."

"You saw him on Friday night," Julia recalled. "For the meeting?"

"Yes, and I wasn't the only one there," Hilda

replied, a faint frown creasing her forehead. "You're not suggesting that I—"

"Of course not, Hilda," Julia assured her. "I was just going to ask how he seemed to you."

Hilda let out a sigh, releasing the tension that had built within her. "Good, because word has spread around the estate about him breaking into my home. I've already received calls from three people asking if I know what happened to him, as if I had something to do with it." Her voice rose, her frustration clear. "And as I mentioned last night, he avoided looking at me all Friday night, but he acted fine with Georgiana and Audrey. He didn't appear ill at all."

"Was anyone else present?"

Hilda shook her head. "No, but that doesn't mean he was poisoned there, does it?"

"No, you're right."

"Julia, I hate to put you in this position," Hilda whispered, drawing closer and grasping Julia's hand, "but if you're as skilled as your gran says you are, will you look into what happened to Ronnie? I don't care about the break-in anymore. I just want whoever did this to be brought to justice."

Julia hesitated, contemplating the weight of Hilda's request. "I can't guarantee anything, but if there is anything I can do, I'll need your help, Hilda. I need to know everything you know about Ronnie and his relationships."

"Thank you, Julia. Thank you so much."

Julia handed Hilda a fresh page in her notepad along with a pen, hiding her earlier heading. As Hilda jotted down names with a renewed sense of hope, Julia observed in silence, glad she had some of her energy back from their last meeting. When Hilda finished, she looked up and crammed the pen lid back with determination.

"We'll see each other at the food bank tomorrow?"

Julia nodded, not knowing how she could turn down the invitation. "Yes, we will."

With Audrey waiting for her, Hilda hurried off into the rain, and Julia's thoughts turned inward, her mind brimming with the weight of what she'd just agreed to. Raindrops continued their concerto outside, the allure of the banana bread recipe fading against the backdrop of something bigger.

Pen hovering over the paper, Julia hesitated at the creaking open of the dining room door. Barker followed Mowgli into the kitchen, his gaze drifting over Julia's shoulder at the notes Hilda had scribbled.

"'Paige. Run-ins with the next-door neighbour,'" Barker read aloud, wrapping an arm around Julia's shoulder. "And 'Norman. Brother, bad blood.' Interesting."

Julia nodded, her eyes scanning the list. "I have a few more names to add. Georgiana, a volunteer at the food bank, didn't hide her lack of sadness over Ronnie's death. And Audrey, another volunteer, went to school with him, so she might have valuable insights."

"You're talking like you've taken the case on."

Julia hesitated, her pen gliding across the page as Barker washed his coffee cup and rested it on the straining board. He leaned against the breakfast bar, glancing at Julia's notes upside down while peeling a blackened banana, revealing its ripe interior with only a few darkened patches.

"Not to stir things up," Barker mumbled through a mouthful of mushed banana, "but that man handing out flyers had a lot to say about Hilda when he saw you talking to her."

"Did you catch his name?" Julia inquired, jotting down the note.

"No, but he made a point of mentioning that Hilda used to work for the council. He called her a 'master of spin,' like she shouldn't be trusted as much as she was."

"All that from handing out a flyer?"

"Could be nothing," he said, planting a kiss on her cheek. "I've finished writing for the day, so I'll meet you in bed. Don't stay up too late."

After sprinkling some cat treats for Mowgli at the end of the breakfast bar, Julia tapped her pen against the pad as distant thunder rumbled outside. The mention of the mysterious flyer man's comments about Hilda added another layer of intrigue. However, Julia didn't believe that Hilda could be the one who poisoned her dear friend just because she worked for the council in the past. The Fern Moore community relied on Hilda's service, and with Ronnie, the sole reason for keeping the food bank afloat—according to *The Peridale Post*'s profile that she'd got around to reading—the people would need Hilda more than ever.

The banana bread could wait until the morning.

Feeling the weight of Hilda's wobbling reputation baring down on her, Julia returned her attention to the original page with the heading. With the information she knew about Ronnie and the clues unfolding before her, she allowed her pen to work its magic.

~

Across the lane, with the warm rain continuing to pound down long into the night, Jessie ducked under Veronica's arm as she ushered her into her cottage.

Stacked boxes lined the hallway, a temporary barricade of belongings yet to find their place.

"Ignore the mess," Veronica said, nudging a box aside to clear more of the path. "I swear, unpacking is feeling like an eternal punishment, but I'm sure I'll get around to it when I have a second to breathe. Don't suppose you know anything about tending to roses?"

"Sorry, not my thing. Your last day at the college should be coming up soon?"

Veronica's eyes gleamed. "Two more weeks, and then I'm free."

Manoeuvring through the cardboard obstacle course, Jessie followed Veronica into the kitchen. Aside from the boxes, the cottage was still pristine from Leah and Johnny's last days there. Its modern show-home trimmings of grey, gold, and navy blue were a far cry from Julia's cosy cottage across the lane, but the décor didn't seem to match Veronica's colourful nature either. A slew of red ink-tainted coursework covered the breakfast bar, the only suggestion of anything personal. Veronica climbed onto a stool and picked up the pen, letting Jessie know what she'd interrupted.

Leaning against the counter, Jessie asked, "So, got a big retirement bash planned?"

"I'll be more than happy leaving through the back

door. Teaching was never my dream job. I just got a little stuck."

"And journalism was your dream?"

"I didn't have a dream," she muttered, crossing out an entire section with harsh red lines. "I always enjoyed reading, so I studied English Literature and Language at university, and when my old friend, Michelle, said she was doing her teacher training, I thought, 'Why not?'" She glanced up with a wry smile. "Reckless, I know. Michelle fell in love with Michael, and it wasn't long before they shipped off to New Zealand to start a new life, and well...here I am, sixty-five, having figured out what I want to do. And with coursework like this, it couldn't come at a better time." She cleared her throat and read, "'Atticus Finch filled Boo Radley's tree hole with cement because he didn't like trees.' I mean, it's a wonder I survived as a teacher for *this* long. I don't know whether to laugh or cry." She let out a sound somewhere between the two. Looking up at Jessie, she added, "My quotes?"

Jessie rubbed her arm. "I didn't get any. Did you hear about what happened?"

"It's one of my jobs to know," she said with that same smile again. "Already published an article about it, but I'm a little light on the facts. The police are saying it looks like poison. What the police haven't said is that he was likely killed with ricin. You can thank my hospital porter contact for that."

"Ricin?"

"You're the one studying biology, you tell me."

"Funnily enough, I didn't learn about ricin on the syllabus." In the mess of coursework clutter, Jessie spotted listings printed from an estate agent's website. "You're moving already? No wonder you haven't got around to unpacking."

"It's for the newspaper. Cotswold Media Group, in their infinite wisdom, dumped all the local papers together in a single building miles away when they bought everyone out years ago. The place is falling apart. Some old relic from the seventies that springs a new leak every time they fix one. I think I'm in with a shot of moving operations back to the village."

"You think they'll go for it? Johnny always made it seem like there was no budging them on anything."

That wry smile again. "Johnny was a pushover. I am not. The only language they speak is money, so if I can find somewhere that saves them money, I can't see why they'd refuse." She tossed the pen down and leaned back, taking Jessie in. "So, you didn't get me any quotes, and yet you still came to see me. What's eating you up? Something tells me it's not exam nerves for tomorrow?"

While Veronica peeled a satsuma, Jessie considered telling her about her run-in with Billy. But what would it achieve? It had been two years since Billy left Peridale in search of a new life in the army, so it wasn't like her tutor, who'd only known her since the start of the year, could offer any advice.

Not that she needed any.

Seeing her ex meant nothing, even if it had stopped her in her tracks.

"I left this part out when you came to see me last night, but I knew Ronnie once upon a time," Jessie said instead, turning down an offer of a satsuma segment. "I can't believe I'm telling you this, but I used to live on the streets, and so did Ronnie. We hung around the same industrial park, and he wasn't all that nice back then."

"I know." Veronica's smile turned sympathetic. "About you being homeless, I mean."

"How, I never—"

"You wrote about it in your personal statement when you applied to the college," she said between mouthfuls. "The orphaned girl who'd slept rough and yet somehow found a family in this sleepy little village. The girl who'd found her long-lost brother and travelled the world with him, only to come home to realise she didn't know who she was or what she wanted out of life, all she knew was that she didn't want to go backwards."

Jessie was a little taken aback, not sure whom she'd thought would read what she'd written in her application after those espresso martinis at the wedding, but her English tutor hadn't been one of them.

"No need to look so embarrassed," Veronica whispered. "It's one of the better ones I've read. You've come a long way since then, Jessie. You should be proud of that."

"Yeah, well, maybe I still don't know where I'm going." Shrugging, Jessie pulled the ID from her pocket and tossed it onto the abandoned coursework. "Maybe I never will."

Veronica glanced at the ID, then back at Jessie. "And maybe journalism isn't your calling, maybe it is, but it's a starting point," she said, pushing the ID back. "Because I know if you were content working at the café for the rest of your life, you wouldn't be here right now. Now, if you don't mind, I have more of Ben's two-month late *To Kill a Mockingbird* analysis to suffer through, and I cannot wait to see what other riveting observations he's made about my favourite book. Fern Moore—that's your starting point for digging into Ronnie's story."

Sighing, Jessie said, "Why can't you do it?"

"Because I'm one woman trying to do a million and one things."

"The paper must have other reporters?"

"Two, and neither live in Peridale."

"How does that even work?"

"It doesn't," Veronica said through the last of her satsuma before scooping the pen up. "You know the area, and I haven't made myself popular there since I took over the paper. I may have barged in waving my badge around a little too much. Jessie, I need your help," she whispered, her tone dropping an octave. "So, are you in?"

~

For the second night in a row, a shadow outside the cottage made Julia's heart stop in its tracks. She was about to call out for Barker when the sound of a key turning in the lock of the front door stopped her.

Unlike Hilda and Ronnie, she didn't keep a spare under the doormat, and as far as she knew, there were only two other keys to the front door floating around the village. Julia would have fine seeing her gran, even at this late hour, but she was relieved when Jessie slipped into the hallway from the rain.

"Hey, Mum," Jessie whispered, glancing through

the open door of the starry-lit nursery that used to be her bedroom. "I saw the light on and hoped one of you would be awake. Don't tell Dad, but I'm glad it's you. How's his book coming along?"

Julia raised a finger to her lips, and they shared a soft laugh at Barker's snoring. "Well enough that he's asleep long before me tonight. Turns out there's nothing like a fresh murder to unblock a blocked writer. Burning the midnight oil with your revision?"

"Yeah." Jessie pulled Julia into a hug, and her daughter needed it, but Julia needed it just as much. "How are you?"

"Fine," she said, before amending, "No, I'm not fine."

"And I'm not up studying."

"But you have been revising?" Julia pulled away from the hug. "Your exam is tomorrow."

"Thanks for the reminder. I had no idea." A sarcastic laugh settled Julia's worry. "What's going on?"

"Did you hear about the man they found at Fern Moore?"

Jessie nodded, pulling away from the hug and allowing Julia to see how tired her daughter was up close.

"I found him," Julia admitted with a sigh. "Along

with the owner of the food bank, Hilda. It wasn't a pleasant afternoon, to be honest."

"Wait?" Jessie peered down her nose. "So, you knew Ronnie too?"

Julia mirrored Jessie's confusion. "Too?"

"I'd better fill the kettle," Jessie said, already making her way to the kitchen as if she had never moved out. "Seems like we both have some explaining to do."

With steaming cups of peppermint and liquorice tea in hand, they settled in the sitting room. As the wind and rain whistled down the chimney, they exchanged their stories about Ronnie, and Julia was more than a little surprised to learn that her daughter's knowledge of Ronnie extended further back than her own or Hilda's.

"So, he was a thief back then as well?" Julia pondered when her teacup was halfway empty. "It seems he served in the army for a while, was homeless for a time, and then somehow ended up living on the estate to become the saviour of the food bank."

"And now he's dead."

"Something doesn't add up." Julia glanced across the darkened hall to the bedroom where Barker's snores had taken on a primal grunt. "Listen, Jessie, keep this between us, but I might look into the murder. For Hilda's sake, and only if the police don't come up with something, which they will."

"They care less about the Fern Moore stuff," Jessie claimed, although Julia wasn't sure if that was true. "But there's something else. Something else happened today..."

Jessie fell silent long enough for Julia to notice that the rain had stopped for the first time all night. Staring into her peppermint tea, her daughter seemed burdened with the weight of the world on her shoulders. Julia reached out and rested a hand on Jessie's knee, prompting a smile from her, though it didn't ease the knot of maternal worry.

"I said I would look into things for Veronica," Jessie said, a little lighter. "For the newspaper."

"Oh."

"If you don't want me to, I—"

Julia let out a laugh. "From your expression just now, I thought something else had happened. Unless—"

"No, nothing else." Jessie finished the rest of her tea in one gulp. "Nothing important. So, it's settled then. We're both looking into this, so I suppose I'll see you at Fern Moore tomorrow?"

"Already planned to be there."

It was Jessie's turn to laugh, though it twisted into a yawn. "I should have known you'd already be all over it. I need to get to bed if I want to be alert during my exam tomorrow."

"The sofa's yours if you want it."

Jessie considered the offer but shook her head. "I'll leave you and the snoring supremo alone. Makes me glad I live alone."

"I'm not sure what's worse—the nights he snores after a productive writing session, or the nights he tosses and turns, trying to think of a plot twist to get unstuck." They hugged, and Julia felt Jessie hold on a little longer than usual during a goodbye hug. "If there's anything else, I'm always here."

"I know. It's nothing important." After a last squeeze, Jessie let go. "What's important now is finding out who killed Ronnie and why they'd want to."

Julia stood by the front door until Jessie's yellow Mini disappeared around the bend in the dark lane. After locking the doors and checking on Olivia one last time, Julia considered going over her notes again, but she decided they could wait until breakfast. She followed Mowgli into the bedroom and shook Barker from his snoring as she climbed into bed, wanting to be as clear minded as possible tomorrow. She had a crate of overripe bananas to turn into banana bread, and she needed to decide who she wanted to speak to first.

Closing her eyes, one of her gran's observations came to mind, deciding for her. It *had* been odd that Georgiana seemed more concerned about touching up her makeup than the loss of one of her fellow volunteers.

6

Leaving Barker with a full French press of coffee and his laptop in the dining room and dropping Olivia off at the nursery for her scheduled play morning, Julia headed to the café with the bananas and her notepad. Although she was eager to review her Ronnie notes, she spent the first ten minutes sipping her favourite minty tea at the stainless-steel counter while she prepared her mother's banana bread recipe:

250g of all-purpose flour
1 teaspoon of baking soda
113g of unsalted butter, softened
200g of granulated sugar
2 large eggs
4 ripe bananas, mashed

60ml of milk

A generous pinch of salt

A splash of vanilla extract

A dash of cinnamon

A handful of chopped walnuts (optional)

Peeling forty-eight bananas and mashing them into a bowl, she multiplied the recipe to take it from one loaf to twelve. Although bulk baking wasn't her preferred method, Julia embraced the task. She whisked three kilograms of flour with the baking soda and salt and creamed every tub of butter with almost all the café's white sugar. She beat twenty-four eggs into the wet mixture one by one, her expert hand leaving not a trace of the shells. Next, she added the mashed bananas, combined everything with milk, and added the crucial vanilla extract and cinnamon. For those with allergies, she skipped the walnuts. She poured the batter into twelve of the café's fifteen loaf tins and stacked them in the giant oven.

The baking loaves filled the kitchen with their rich sweet aroma while Julia placed a delivery order at the cash and carry. She also prepared batter for some simple sponges, using coconut oil instead of butter and brown sugar instead of white. Sue arrived to open the café on what promised to be a quiet Monday as Julia sliced the last of the twelve loaves into ten individual pieces. She wrapped each slice in a wax paper square before placing them in leftover cardboard boxes.

"Your challenge, should you choose to accept it," Julia said, closing the boot of her car with a thud after Sue helped her load the boxes, "is to figure out a way to sell those coconut oil cakes by the end of the day without making it obvious they're backups."

"And if I can't?"

"Then I'll have no choice but to fire you and hire Gran instead," Julia replied with a quick kiss on Sue's cheek on the café's doorstep. "The delivery should arrive before noon. Good luck."

"Same to you, Miss Marple," Sue said, handing Julia her small notepad. "You wouldn't want to forget this."

No, she wouldn't.

With just a sliver of a view through her rear-view mirror over the top of her packed backseats, Julia set off for Fern Moore under a cheerful, cloudless sky. Her morning at the café clearing out the supplies had filled her with optimism for the day ahead. She pulled into the quiet car park, and after a quick scan of her notes, she felt the same as when she'd drifted off to sleep the night before.

Georgiana was the obvious person to speak to first.

In the courtyard, gangs loitered in front of the shops, while the park echoed with the laughter of toddlers and their parents. In the shadowy alley of the food bank, Audrey and Hilda were raising the shutters. Julia noticed them and waved, pointing to the boxes. Audrey retrieved a shopping trolley from the storage unit and rushed over with a muttered greeting.

"You gave me forty-eight bananas," Julia said, loading the boxes into the rusty trolley. "I give you one hundred and twenty slices of banana bread."

"Yes, very well done," Audrey replied, stealing a glance at her watch. "We have a busy day ahead of us."

"Things are different around here compared to yesterday. Almost back to business as usual," Julia remarked.

"People have their own troubles to deal with," Audrey said, spinning the trolley around and setting off. Julia locked her car and hurried to catch up. Audrey continued, "As tragic as the incident was, life must go on. I'm confident the police will provide answers soon enough. Meanwhile, we have yesterday's backlog to tackle and today's home deliveries."

Although Hilda had visited Julia's cottage the previous evening, begging for Julia's help for the second night in a row, her enthusiasm for Julia's investigative presence seemed diminished. Together with Audrey, she declined the offer of sampling the banana bread, insisting that they should only be for the parcels. Hilda kept Julia occupied by sorting the shelves from the moment the first person entered the unit. It may not have been Julia's reason for being there, but she made herself useful. After an hour of rearranging, following the café's system of placing lighter items on lower shelves and keeping heavier cans at reachable levels, Julia brought some order to the cluttered rows, doubling the shelf space.

"How many donations do you think we get?" Audrey snapped when Julia showed her the progress. "But yes, I suppose it looks neater. Have you heard from Georgiana, Hilda? She's usually here by now, and I need to get the deliveries out."

"I can't think about that girl right now," Hilda replied, busy at the counter with the line already snaking out of the shutters. "But it's not like her to miss a day. In fact, she hasn't missed a single day since she first turned up here."

"Maybe I scared her off yesterday? Good riddance, I say."

Hilda hesitated and said, "Her heart is in the right place."

"Is it?"

"She's volunteered more hours than any of us."

"Only because she can," Audrey said with a sigh, tossing the wrapped banana bread into the boxes like a suitcase being flung onto an airport conveyor belt.

"If I had my father's credit card, I'd be here every hour too. But some of us need to work to pay the bills. Speaking of which, I need to be out of here by two, and you know people call by noon when we're late with the deliveries."

"Then let's hope she turns up."

"You could call her?" Julia suggested. "Is she local?"

Audrey and Hilda both shrugged, leaving Julia to wonder what had happened in the night for their attitudes to have taken such a turn. She'd been hoping to start her investigation with Georgiana, and if not her, Ronnie's biggest cheerleader or his old school acquaintance. Audrey wasn't acting too different from the first time Julia had met her, focused only on the job at hand, but Hilda seemed to be actively avoiding her.

If Julia was going to be filling Georgiana's shoes for the day, she would make herself more useful than rearranging shelves to look as neat as possible. She picked up the itinerary Audrey had abandoned on a chair.

"I can start on the home deliveries," Julia offered, a little afraid to interrupt their well-oiled double act. "I know my way around the place well."

"I always do deliveries," Audrey replied. "People know my face."

"Julia's not a stranger to this community, and I need you here," Hilda said, flapping a finger at a shopping trolley. "Ronnie fished it out of the canal. You'll need to make a couple of trips, but you'll be able to manage a cartload per floor if you stack them right."

Audrey gave a conceding sigh and said, "Just tick them off as you go. You'll lose track otherwise."

More than used to dealing with keeping track of orders and stock levels in the café, Julia went down the long list of people booked in for home deliveries, using the guides on the wall to pack boxes for singles, couples, and families. There was a varied mix of all three, but the number of families with multiple 'dependents' alarmed Julia. Of all her worries about how she spent her time juggling the café with raising Olivia and finding time to have a life outside of work and motherhood, Julia never had to worry about how she was going to feed her family. Even if Barker didn't have his income from the PI cases and royalties from his first book, she would have coped with the café's earnings to keep both hers and Olivia's bellies full.

"We don't have time for waterworks," Audrey huffed as Julia dabbed at her eyes with a handkerchief. "Are you getting the deliveries out or not?"

"I am. It's just a lot to process."

"So, process it and get on with what needs doing."

"Cut her some slack, Audrey," Hilda whispered over her shoulder, offering Julia her first smile since the three of them arrived. "Remember why we started this charity? You were once just as shocked, and that was when demand was half what it is now. If it's too much, Julia, we can always—"

Julia cleared her throat. "I'm fine. I'll be back soon."

Chalking the tension in the storage unit up to grief and exhaustion, Julia pushed the trolley across the courtyard, trying to refocus her thoughts on the task at hand. She'd start on the top floor, beginning with Norman Roberts' flat, labelled as 102. Hoping that the lift had been repaired overnight, she pressed the lift button, but the graffitied metal doors didn't respond.

"Out of order, I'm afraid," a soft and husky voice called. "That's quite a substantial shopping trip you've got there. Please don't tell me I'll have to arrest you for stealing a supermarket trolley. We take such high-level crimes very seriously."

Julia turned to see Detective Inspector Laura Moyes, her dark blonde hair gleaming in the sun. She wore a grey silk blouse tucked into black skinny-leg trousers. After the disheartening hour spent in the storage unit, Julia was relieved to see a familiar face, despite Laura's piercing gaze as she glanced over her chic sunglasses.

"Property of the food bank, via a canal," Julia explained. "So, recycling?"

"Ah, I'll let you off this time, though I can't help but be suspicious seeing you so close to my crime scene two days in a row. Wouldn't be snooping around, would you, Julia?"

Julia shared a smile with the detective. "Me? Snooping? Never."

"You're as good a liar as your grandmother."

"She wouldn't be shouting at you in the street, would she?"

"No, but she wouldn't let me enjoy a peaceful late breakfast in your café with Roxy without barking endless questions about the investigation at me. Apparently, we have some competition. So, I guessed it was you or your husband."

"I thought you were the DI over in Riverswick?"

"I am," she said with a huff. "But Peridale has been 'too quiet' since they sacked DI Christie over that festival case blundering, so they're not in a rush to waste their resources. Why would they, when they can keep dragging me over to sort your messes out? And here I was thinking I was moving from cold cases to the Cotswolds for an easier life." She looked around the estate before settling on the trolley. "Not to pass judgement on your strength, but I don't think you're going to win the battle with the stairs with that thing."

"I think you're right. But since you're here—"

"Not a chance." Laura stepped back and looked up to the second floor, making eye contact with a young police constable in full uniform. "Your husband has been pestering me for my personal notes on the capsule cold case. And considering how little time he has left for the occasional drink PI to DI drink these days, I assume his new book is going well?"

"If he's anything like when I left him, he's writing up a storm at home."

"Then I'll leave you in PC Puglisi's capable hands," Laura said as the panting officer descended the stairwell. "And I apologise in advance. Ah! Jake, help this lovely lady carry the shopping trolley up the steps, will you? Which floor, Julia?"

"Third."

"Third?" PC Jake Puglisi looked up, letting out a sigh with his hands on his hips. "Wait, did you say Julia? As in Barker Brown's wife, Julia?"

By the time they had lugged the trolley up to the first floor, Julia understood Laura's apology. PC Puglisi seemed to be around Jessie's age and appeared to be the biggest Barker Brown fan, bombarding Julia with questions about the follow-up book. While Julia hadn't undergone media training like her husband during his one and only press tour, her days spent avoiding gossip in the café made her an expert in vague and polite responses. By the second floor, Jake seemed to get the hint that she wouldn't reveal plot details, but it didn't dampen his enthusiasm for gushing about Barker's first book, *The Girl in the Basement*. By the time they reached the third floor, Julia knew Jake's mother's name was Glinda, his dog was Rollo, and he had been a responding officer at her café after the unfortunate book club murder.

"Thank you, Jake. I can manage from here."

"Before you go," he whispered, beckoning Julia closer. "Do you think you could get me a signed copy when he's finished?"

Assuring him she would make it happen and expressing her gratitude once more, Julia hurried down the walkway, contemplating how lightly she would need to pack the trolley to manage her next trip alone.

Going door to door to those on her list, the reactions varied from suspicion to gratitude to embarrassment, but Julia maintained her smile throughout and promised everyone there was an extra sweet treat in their food box, which seemed to brighten a few faces. When she reached Norman's flat, she was ready to delve deeper into Ronnie's death, only to be met with open curtains revealing an empty flat and no instructions on what to do with the parcel if the recipient was absent.

"If you're looking for Norman, he left about an hour ago," a woman passing by with shopping bags informed Julia. "Knowing him, he's wasting his money in a slot machine."

"Thank you. Do you know where?"

"Take your pick."

The woman retreated into a nearby flat, leaving Julia to look down at the courtyard. She didn't have to look far to find evidence of slot machines. There was one in the café and another in the barbershop, both vacant despite their alluring flickering lights. She made a mental note to monitor them and finished her third-floor deliveries, wondering if she was going to get any chances to talk to any of the suspects soon.

7

Frozen behind the wheel of her Mini in the car park at Fern Moore, Jessie tried to make heads or tails of how she'd done in her exam as she scrolled through the effects of ricin poisoning on her phone.

Veronica had been waiting outside the sports hall at the college before Jessie walked in, assuring her she would do great and that by the time the exam was over, Jessie would know whether she'd passed or failed. She didn't know. All she knew was that it had been hard. Harder than chemistry and physics, and somehow harder than maths. And that one had made her cry out of frustration.

The section asking her to describe the process of photosynthesis had been the easiest part, and she had completely blanked on what cell mitosis even was. But it was the question about poisons that had stuck with her:

'Pick a common poison and explain how it acts as a toxin in the body, including its potential mode of entry, target organs or tissues, and the symptoms it produces.'

If Jessie had read the article about how ricin is a 'potent protein derived from the castor bean plant and affected organs rich in blood supply, such as the liver, kidneys, spleen, and lungs', she might have scored full marks for that question and left feeling satisfied she'd known something.

The thought of Ronnie dying like that in his chair drove her out of the car, with Veronica's advice from when Jessie had left the exam hall pushing forward.

"Be *bold*, Jessie," Veronica had said before sending her on her way to Fern Moore. "If we get this scoop before the police, it's going to show the people with the money that there's still value in a competent local paper."

Veronica cared about impressing the men with the money.

Jessie cared about finding out the truth.

Locking her car with a click of her keys, she set off for Daphne's Café, ready to shake down whoever was inside to find out anything she could about the suspects pulled from her mum's list. She was eager to learn more about Hilda without her mum's obvious bias about the 'sweet old lady' routine.

According to an article Jessie had found that morning instead of last-minute cramming about mitosis and poisons, Hilda had retired from the council's planning department a year before she started the food bank charity with four other women. Janis, a lawyer, and Trudy, a fellow councilwoman, both died within a year of each other from natural causes shortly after the food bank opened. Ronnie's old school pal, Audrey, was a part-time social worker and part-time volunteer. Jessie had dealt with her fair share of social workers growing up in the care system, but their paths had never crossed.

Walking into the café with its bright orange walls and exposed industrial ceiling, all intentions of being bold vanished in an instant. Jessie almost turned around at the sight of Billy behind the counter in a wall-matching orange apron. But as their eyes met, everything seemed to freeze for a moment. If it weren't for those blue eyes, she would have recognised Billy even less than she had yesterday when he was being pushed into a police car with a balaclava framing his face.

"Jessie..."

"They released you then," was all she could bring herself to say. "Hi, Billy."

"Let off with a caution. Jessie, I—" he started, and she was relieved to see he seemed just as nervous as she felt. "You look great."

Billy grinned, revealing a tooth far back on the right that hadn't been missing before. And that wasn't all. He looked older, the shaved head not helping. He had always been a year older than her, but now he really looked it, like the boy she had known had been swallowed up by a man who had spent much of the last two years lifting heavy things, judging by the width of his shoulders and arms.

"So," she said, rocking back on her heels as she took in the café. They were alone aside from an older man half-asleep by the slot machine. "Going to guess you're not in the army anymore?" She gestured at a lion tattoo roaring on the side of his neck, and he nodded. "How long have you been back?"

"About a month."

"I tried to call you a few times," she said, not entirely sure why. "You didn't pick up."

"Changed my number." He looked down at the ground, something he used to do when he didn't know what to say. "So, are you still at the café?"

"Part-time. Just finished a six-month stint at college. Sat my last GCSE this morning."

There was that grin again. "Oh yeah? I'm well proud of you. You always used to say you regretted not trying harder at school. You're moving up in the world, babe."

Jessie flinched. Nobody had called her 'babe' since he left. It had started as cute when they first got together, annoying by the end.

"You're working in a café," she pointed out, stuck for anything else to say. "Bet you never thought that would happen?"

"A lot of things happened I didn't think would." He fixed on her, his stare as cold as ice, but a blink snapped him back in an instant. "So, what are you after? A coffee? Sandwich? Daphne makes the best sandwiches, all fresh. I'm probably due a break soon. We could catch up. Properly, I mean."

"Another time, maybe?" Jessie said, wishing she hadn't seen the disappointment drop over his face. "I'm actually here on business."

"Café business?"

"Newspaper business. Favour for a friend, but I'm looking into what happened to Ronnie. I sort of knew him, and—"

"Me too," Billy cut in, looking out to the flats. "I've been living next door to him since I got back. Poor guy. I would hear him waking up, shouting in the middle of the night."

"Shouting at who?"

"Ghosts," Billy said, his gaze distant for a moment before snapping back to the old man by the machine that hadn't stopped chirping since Jessie had entered the café. "Norman over there was Ronnie's brother, but I'm not sure you'll get much out of him. He shouted the police away when they tried an hour ago. Doesn't look like he slept much last night, not that it ever does." The old man next to the machine glared at her. She offered him a smile, but he returned it with a blank stare. "He's mostly fine. Did Hilda find your mum the other night?"

"How do you know about that?"

"I hope she didn't mind me giving her the address. Hilda was in here asking if anyone knew where to find 'Julia from the village', and I just knew it had to be her. Hilda was in a proper state."

"Do you trust Hilda?"

"Why shouldn't—" Billy stopped abruptly, his eyes darting to the window. "He's got some *nerve*. I'm going to flatten him."

Billy ripped off his apron and moved around the counter, but when Jessie saw the man with the green tie handing out flyers outside, her old instincts kicked in. She reached out and grabbed Billy's thick arm.

"Whatever he's done, it's not worth it," she said firmly. "From what I saw, seems you got lucky with a caution yesterday." He pulled against her grip, but not enough to break her light grasp. "He's not worth it, Billy."

"You don't know what he's up to," he said, going back behind the counter and pacing in front of the coffee machine. "Benedict and people like him are ruining the community that was here."

"Places change. Time moves on."

"Nah, Jessie," he said, still pacing. "You don't get it. Benedict Langley is a pure slimeball. He's *forcing* Fern Moore to move on regardless of if the people 'round here want it. Handing out those flyers day and night, offering people way undervalue to buy their flats from under them, and people are so desperate for cash right now, they're selling up and scattering, and the flats he's bought are just sitting there empty like he's waiting to do something with them." He stopped pacing and tossed a finger toward the window. "And *he's* not the only one. They've left this place alone for years, but now developers are snapping up these flats and selling them for double what they paid. Everyone's rents are rocketing. This place has always had its problems, but it used to be a last stop before the streets for people who couldn't afford anywhere else."

"It was better when the council used to own this whole place," Norman spoke up with a bitter lilt to his gruff voice, now throwing coins into the slot machine. "I've been here since the start, and they stopped caring about us almost as soon as they built it. They've been selling it off chunk by chunk ever since. Washed their hands of folk like us years ago."

Sensing an opportunity, Jessie left Billy at the counter and approached the slot machine. Judging by his wrinkles and patchy white stubble, Norman was somewhere in his seventies. He huffed at her as she leaned on the machine, but she held her ground.

"Ronnie was your brother," she stated.

"Yeah, and I'll tell you what I told the police. I couldn't give a rat's behind that he's dead." Despite his bitter words, she picked up on a shake in his voice. Another coin went into the machine. "Sorry good-for-nothing. He only ever thought about himself. He could have helped me all this time, but no. Ronnie cared about Ronnie."

"Have some respect, or get out," Billy called, surprising both of them. "You don't know what he went through."

Norman grumbled something under his breath and said, "He always had a sob story to tell. He could have helped me, couldn't he?"

"Helped you how?" Jessie asked, not liking Norman one bit. "Like you helped him when he was living on the streets, you mean?"

He grumbled again. "That was his choice. Look how he ended up."

"I don't think he asked to be poisoned," she said, examining the grumpy old man. "Ricin, they're saying. Someone must have given it to him on Friday. Got yourself an alibi, Norman?"

He paused, offering no reaction to the poisoning revelation as his fingers jabbed at the machine's many buttons. "I was at home. All day." He dug in his pocket and fed in two coins, one after the other. "He could have given me some of that money, but no. Not Ronnie. Never looked out for his own. Back in my day, cowards weren't rewarded when they quit the army."

"That's enough," Billy ordered, slapping a hand on the counter. "Don't make me ask twice, Norman. *Out.*"

Another coin went into the machine, but when it didn't spit out any winnings, Norman tossed a hand gesture at the counter as he shuffled out and further down the row of shops.

"He doesn't know what he's talking about," Billy spat, still seething. "*No* idea. Ronnie did his best for people around here. Ask around about Norman because *everyone* has his cards marked. Gambles away his pension on the first week of every month, and then he's begging and borrowing to get by until the next lot comes in. And don't believe a thing about Norman being home all day on Friday. I saw him at Platts

Social Club across the way around lunchtime, hogging their machine and snapping at anyone who asked for their turn. Ronnie was troubled, but he wasn't trouble."

Jessie almost mentioned that she had known Ronnie as being trouble back in the day, but she stopped herself. If he had received a substantial army payout that made Norman as jealous as he was, she couldn't understand why Ronnie had chosen to linger around the industrial park. She almost asked Billy if he knew why, but he was back to staring out the window with that distant look, paying no attention to Benedict as he captured the attention of a young couple pushing a pram.

"A drink," Billy blurted out. "Let me take you for a drink. I saw that new bar in Peridale when they let me out this morning. What do you say?"

"Billy, I'm not sure I—"

"Just for a catch-up," he said quickly, holding his hands up. "I want to get to know this new Jessie. You seem different. In a good way, I mean."

Jessie wanted to say the same for Billy, but she wasn't sure. In some ways, he was still that kid from the estate who had run off to the army to find himself. That same kid who was too quick to use his fists at the first sign of trouble. But from the far-off look in his eyes, Ronnie wasn't the only one with ghosts.

"For a catch-up," she confirmed. "My phone number's still the same if you still have it."

He offered a shy smile, one eye squinted. "Yeah, I know. Sorry if I freaked you out the other night. Heard your voice and didn't know what to say. I guess fate had other ideas, right?"

After a promise that he'd send her a text about the drink, she left Billy to his quiet Monday in the café. Jessie didn't believe in fate or if a drink at Richie's would truly be just for a catch-up, but she was glad to know who the mystery caller had been. What she believed in, however, was finding out the truth, and she was willing to be bold.

Clearing her throat, she tapped Benedict Langley on the shoulder and plastered on her best smile, tinged with enough worry that his eyes lit up when he spun around.

"Excuse me, sorry to bother you, but did I hear you say you offer instant cash?" Jessie asked in her best 'little girl lost' voice. The greedy grin pricking up his cheeks turned her stomach. "It's just, my Uncle Ronnie died yesterday. They're saying he was murdered. You might have known him. He was a volunteer at that food bank down there. I think he might have left his flat to me in his will. But I'm not sure I want to live in it after what happened to him there. I have this boyfriend, and he's afraid of ghosts, and I don't want to scare him off if my poor Uncle Ronnie is haunting the place."

"You young *love birds* deserve a perfect place, but first, let me just say how *deeply* sorry for your loss. I'm afraid I didn't know your uncle," Benedict said, bowing his head slightly, his black hair as oily as his shiny face. "But what I know is that you were right about what you heard. Instant cash guaranteed. Now, if you wouldn't mind, why don't we take a seat on that fine bench over there, and I can tell you all about how I can take care of your dear Uncle Ronnie's flat."

~

Once back at the food bank, Julia was relieved that the second floor had half the number of deliveries. Hilda and Audrey seemed satisfied with her quick return—or weren't as snappy, at least—and she was soon out again for the second round. Convincing herself that it was no different from pulling Olivia's pram up that flight of stairs at the hospital when their lifts were being serviced during her last check-up, Julia bumped the trolley full of clattering jars and clinking cans up to the second floor and wasted no time making her way down the list.

Julia knocked on the door of Paige's flat, and peering through the open door of Ronnie's flat was the last thing she wanted to do. Curiosity got the better of her. She had been trying to forget the image of the lifeless man sitting in the armchair, staring blankly at the TV. The armchair was gone, the television off, but the haunting image lingered like an unsettled ghost. Julia hoped that the officers meticulously searching the scene would find what they were looking for.

"She won't answer," DI Laura Moyes called from inside the flat before stepping out, a pained expression on her face, her hands on her lower back. She leaned against the concrete barrier, gazing down as Julia knocked again. "No, really. She won't answer. Not as long as we're here. We've been trying all morning and barely got more than 'dunno' and 'maybe' from her last night, but we know she's in there." Laura's voice grew louder, and Julia was certain she heard a giggling child followed by shushing from the other side of the door. "But you're only here to deliver a food parcel, right?"

Julia retrieved the package for Paige and her two children and left it on the doorstep. "Exactly."

"So, you wouldn't want to have a look around the crime scene?" Moyes asked, while Julia busied herself with the checklist. She ticked off Paige, added a note about leaving it on the doorstep, and ran her finger to the next name, four flats further down. Laura popped her head into the flat and called, "Everyone out. I'm calling lunch."

The officers needed no convincing to file out, and after DI Moyes thrust a ten-pound note upon PC Puglisi with an order to bring back a coffee with a double shot, Laura offered the flat door to Julia. Hands still clutching the trolley handle, Julia hesitated on the walkway. Sighing, Moyes strode into the room and cleared her throat. Julia wouldn't wait to be asked twice.

"A word of this to anyone, and you'll be the next body being taken out of Fern Moore," Moyes said sternly, though her mouth pricked up at the corners. "I can't say I wouldn't appreciate a fresh set of eyes right now. Forensics got what they needed in the night, and I'm free to release the crime scene at any moment, but it's not like anybody is in a rush to get the keys back."

Julia gave the centre of the room a wide berth, the indents from the armchair still lingering on the carpet. She approached the small mantelpiece above a three-bar electric fire lined with framed photographs. Among pictures taken of groups in dusty deserts posing next to tanks and sand-coloured buildings, there were official uniformed portraits showing a man more groomed than she'd have imagined from the rugged man on the front page of the paper.

"Joined the forces when he was seventeen," Moyes said when Julia reached a picture of him looking his youngest, the only one out of uniform. He had his arm around a girl about the same age on a bench, with a fresher Fern Moore in the background. "From the records we found, this was his dad's place. He bought it from the council for dirt cheap in the early nineties. His dad died in 2009 and left Ronnie the flat, and from what we can tell, he rented it out until he came back when he was honourably discharged in 2016."

"He didn't come straight back here," Julia said, turning the frame over. There was no inscription. "He was homeless for a time in late 2016, maybe early 2017. Know who the girl in the picture is?"

"No idea. And how do you know that, and I don't?"

"My daughter," Julia said, settling the picture back. The young couple looked happy. "They frequented the same area. She said he wasn't to be trusted back then."

Moyes pondered the revelation for a moment. "Lines up with the string of offences he racked up around that time. Shoplifting and assault, mostly. There was nothing of note on his record until he was arrested for assault two weeks ago, a fact that seems to have been kept rather quiet around here if the article in the paper is anything to go by. Does the name Benedict Langley ring a bell?"

Julia shook her head, following Moyes' lead into a small, basic bedroom. It was mostly neat, except for the wardrobe, which had an explosion of clothes at the foot that would rival Jessie's flat.

"There was a safe hidden at the bottom, cleared out with the door wide open. Forensics are doing their best to see if they can figure out what was inside it, but there's no way to know if he cleared it out before his death or..."

"His poisoner came in and emptied it out?"

She nodded. "Would be an obvious motive, wouldn't it? Though judging by this place, something tells me Ronnie didn't have a stash of gold bars and a Fabergé egg hidden away. Any thoughts about what could have been in there?"

Julia didn't, and she said as much. "What about the poison? How'd it get in his system?"

"Ingested. There are remnants of three bright blue cupcakes in his stomach and what we think is chicken pie and mashed potatoes. Audrey already confirmed there were cupcakes at their fundraising meeting on Friday, though she couldn't confirm the colour. Said Georgiana always dumped a tray on the table every meeting, so we're eager to speak to her if you know where she is?"

"Didn't turn up to volunteer today, which is apparently a first. Can't you find her address?"

"No house rented or bought in her name, just a silver *Jaguar* convertible, which my officers are busy tracking."

"So, he ingested the ricin. Figure out everyone he saw on Friday—"

"I never said ricin, and there's *no way* you should know that either." The DI's smile was a mix of sour and impressed. "Who's been spilling the beans to you? Does Barker still have old contacts at the Peridale station?"

"*I* have *my* sources," she said, bending to look at the space the safe had been. "If someone came in to enter the safe after he died, were there any signs of the flat being broken into?"

"There was the key under the mat," she said, and after a moment's hesitation, asked, "The old lady. Hilda? How did she know the key was there?"

"She didn't. I suggested it might be."

"And how did you know it would be there?"

"Lucky guess. After what Hilda..." Realising she had said too much, Julia wandered out of the bedroom and back into the sitting room. She stared at the space where the chair had been, a question forming in her mind. "Why take the chair out of here?"

"You're not getting a thing out of me until you finish that sentence." Arms folded, Moyes stared at Julia in a stern pose that would have been threatening if she weren't in the café every other day smooching with Roxy. "You help nobody by keeping secrets."

"I suppose it's not a secret anymore," she said. "Georgiana and Audrey know, and so does my gran, and word is out around the estate."

"Word about what?"

"Ronnie broke into Hilda's home on Friday afternoon," Julia admitted, walking over to the window at the back, looking out over the fields that stretched all the way to the village. "She has proof, but she doesn't know what he took. She didn't want to go to the police because she wanted me to help understand why he would want to do such a thing."

"We've spoken to her twice already. She didn't mention it, so why still keep the secret?"

"Perhaps she doesn't want to tarnish the memory of someone she respected," Julia suggested. "Or maybe she doesn't think it's relevant. It might not be."

Moyes let out a laugh with a condensing edge. "Julia, this changes *everything*. It gives her a clear revenge motive."

Tilting her head, Julia assessed whether the DI was being serious, and by her tightly folded arms, she was. "Why would Hilda bring me here to find the body with her? She was the only person who seemed eager to see him when he didn't show up for the fundraiser yesterday."

"To, I don't know, control the narrative, perhaps?"

Julia's lips parted to counter, but Barker's comment about not trusting Hilda because she was a 'master of spin' rushed to the forefront of her mind. Hilda's change in behaviour that morning from the sweet storybook grandmother she'd met only a few days ago further solidified her silence.

"Regardless, I need to talk to her." Moyes strode over to the door and held it wide open, letting Julia know her time was up. "I'll tell her I heard a whisper on the wind, so the record won't show that you spilt the beans. For someone not investigating this crime, you have a lot to say."

Julia squinted at the picture of the young couple, taking the long way around past the mantelpiece. Their smiles and closeness suggested they were in love, and given their ages, the photo couldn't have been taken long before Ronnie left for the army.

"The chair?"

Sighing, Moyes checked her watch and glanced at the courtyard. "Where's Puglisi with that coffee?"

"The chair, Laura?"

"It's DI Moyes when I'm on the clock," she said, jerking her head at Julia. "And right now, you're trespassing a crime scene, and I think you have bigger fish to fry. Good luck with the rest of your deliveries."

Julia didn't need to wonder if DI Moyes was being serious this time. The moment Julia stepped onto the walkway, DI Moyes pulled the door shut, leaving Julia to stare into the empty trolley that had been half-filled with food parcels when she'd left it. She turned to Paige's flat, and her parcel was gone too. On the other side of the window, she noticed a small white camera perched atop a stack of DVDs.

"I don't suppose you saw anything?" There was giggling and shushing, and Julia let her words fade away before her knuckles reached the wood.

8

Julia dragged the trolley down the stairs with PC Puglisi's help, and she must have looked as shaken up as she felt because the young officer didn't bombard her with more questions. Pushing the trolley across the courtyard, it surprised her to see Jessie talking with the man with a green tie. Jessie caught her eye and made her excuses before rushing off, but not before he thrust some papers upon her. Julia had been wanting to catch him at some point, so she was glad Jessie had.

"How'd your exam go?" Julia asked, noticing Jessie's slumping shoulders at the question. "I'm sure you did fine. Great, even."

"I'm sure we'll see when I get my results at the end

of summer," she replied. "Best to forget all about it, especially with how things are unfolding around here. Found Norman at the café earlier, throwing his pension into a slot machine. You'd think his worst enemy had just died and not his brother."

Two more people than Julia had talked to. "Did he say what Ronnie did to him to make him hate him?"

"Aside from not sharing some money he got from the army, he didn't seem to have any other reasons. He seemed bitter about the entire world, and he lied about his alibi. Said he was at home all day, but Billy said he saw him at Platts Social Club Friday afternoon around lunchtime."

"Mention anything about a chicken pie and mash?"

"Huh?"

"The contents of Ronnie's stomach."

"Oh. Possible ricin delivery?"

"One of them, along with some cupcakes, served at their fundraiser meeting." Julia stopped in her tracks, turning to her daughter. "*Billy?*"

"Your ears work then," Jessie muttered, stopping for a second before marching on towards the food bank. "You just saw me talking to Benedict Langley on that bench just now, and I may have told a white lie about Ronnie being my uncle and leaving his flat to me. He was drooling to make me and my imaginary *love bird* leave Fern Moore for good. Trying to rush me to sign a contract without even giving me time to think about his offer, but at least I now have a copy." She gave the papers a rustle. "My grief might have been fake, but he didn't know that. Total creep."

Julia wasn't ready to move on and slowed Jessie with a hand on her arm. "Billy, as in *your* Billy?"

Jessie sighed, still not immune to a teenage eye roll. "Yes. And he's not *my* Billy. It's not important." She paused and looked back at the café, and Julia remembered Jessie saying something similar when she'd turned up at her cottage in the rain. "Billy thinks Benedict is ruining the community by undervaluing people's flats to get them to move out. Leaving them empty, too. Have you talked to anyone?"

"I had a look around Ronnie's flat," she said. "Jessie, if you want to talk about—"

"I'm talking now, aren't I? I'm fine. Not important. Find anything in Ronnie's flat?"

Julia didn't want to rush past the subject, but she wouldn't push when Jessie didn't want to talk about it. "Just an empty safe and some old photographs. No closer to figuring out what's going on, and to top it off, at least ten food parcels are now missing, thanks to my snooping. I'm dreading going back. Audrey and Hilda weren't the friendliest this morning. I feel like I'm in the way, even though they asked me to be here."

"I asked Benedict about Hilda and he claimed to know nothing about her despite what he said to Dad."

Julia had been so tripped up by hearing her daughter mentioning her ex-boyfriend's name, she'd missed the other familiar name she'd thrown out. "The man with the flyers is Benedict Langley? Did he say anything about Ronnie?"

"Claimed not to have heard of him."

Julia pulled her notepad out and added his name to the list of suspects. "According to DI Moyes, Ronnie assaulted a man called Benedict Langley two weeks ago. I suppose there's a chance Benedict didn't know *who* assaulted him, but it's not like Ronnie was a stranger around here."

"So, two suspects telling two different lies. Did you speak to Georgiana?"

"A no-show, and Paige wouldn't answer the door either."

"And Hilda?"

"Wasn't exactly herself this morning."

"Or maybe she *was* herself and you just fell for a routine the *other* times," Jessie said, ducking into the shadow of the alley opening as a group of teenagers walked past with blaring music. "Look, I know you want to trust her, but just remember what Dad said. Master of spin."

"From Benedict's lips, and he doesn't seem trustworthy either, given what he's just told you."

"Benedict said that to Dad unprompted before any of this started." Checking her phone, Jessie didn't continue down the alley with Julia. "I'll catch you later. Sue said the café is busy and she could use an extra pair of hands."

"On a Monday?"

"Maybe the gossipers know something we don't about Ronnie?" she suggested as she walked away, folding up the contract into her pocket. "Just be on your guard, okay? People aren't always what they seem, even the sweet and charitable old ladies."

Julia waved Jessie off and returned to the food bank with an empty trolley, expecting to be met with a barrage of complaints about letting such a thing happen. To her surprise, the line at the food bank had dried up, and Audrey had gone off to her paying job, leaving only Hilda behind with the graffitied shutter half pulled down. Hilda was enjoying a slice of banana bread. Taking the chair next to her behind the counter, Julia explained the situation.

"It's not your fault, Julia," Hilda said, her snappy tone from earlier softening as she licked crumbs from her lips. "It wouldn't be the first time something like this has happened. At least they didn't threaten you like Audrey the last time they cleared the trolley out.

If you think Paige is behind this, I'll have a word with her. I thought she was the type to keep her nose clean, but I suppose desperate times push people to desperate measures. I'm a little surprised the DI on the case let you into the flat. Did you find anything of note?"

"We're…" Julia almost said 'friends' but stopped herself after her abrupt exit from the scene. "We're acquaintances. Ronnie had an empty safe in his wardrobe. Any idea what he kept in there?"

"To tell you the truth, I hadn't stepped foot in his flat until yesterday, so I knew nothing about a safe," she said before taking her last bite of the banana bread. "You know, I've never been the biggest fan of bananas, but this is divine. And to say you baked as much as you did this morning all off your own back speaks buckets about your character, Julia."

"As long as people enjoy my baking, that's all that matters."

"I'm sure it's brightened up a few people's afternoons, and on reflection," she said, dusting away the crumbs from her floral blouse, "Audrey and I weren't all that polite to you when we first turned up this morning. She asked me to pass on her apologies before she left, and I hope you can accept my apology too. The pressures of this place get to you on any normal day, you see, and I don't have to tell you these have been far from normal days."

"Far from it."

"I don't think either of us slept much last night, and Audrey cares about this food bank and this estate, and if she feels something is getting in the way, she'll do anything she can to put it right." Leaning in, she whispered, "When that group of thugs threatened her for the food last time this happened, she let them for her own safety, of course, but she didn't rest until she'd tracked down every one of them. She gave their names straight to the police, and we didn't get the food back, but it sent out a message we thought had worked. I suppose today proved otherwise. She's a tough cookie, but I think Audrey is taking Ronnie's death harder than she's willing to show. Last night after she drove me home, she was sobbing like your sweet baby girl when I gave her that fright. I had Audrey on my sofa for the night. Didn't want her to be on her own. I didn't want to be on my own, either. I still can't believe someone would want to poison Ronnie."

Julia empathised with the stress Audrey and Hilda were under, especially with the recent events surrounding Ronnie's death. She offered her handkerchief to Hilda to wipe away her fresh tears. "Grief makes people act in strange ways. Are you any closer to figuring out if Ronnie took anything from your house?"

Hilda bowed her head to dab at her inner corners. "I'm not all that invested in finding out anymore given the turn of events, so perhaps it's best we leave that topic be so we can focus on finding out the important things. Who knows, perhaps he was poisoned earlier in the day, and it affected his mind? I'm happy for it to remain a mystery."

Though she wasn't as ready to let the break-in remain a mystery, Julia respected Hilda's decision and changed the subject. Given the person she'd wanted to focus on hadn't turned up, Julia recalled one of the last things she'd heard Georgiana say.

"Last time Georgiana was here, she made a comment about you wanting a 'poster boy' for the paper. Do you know what she meant by that?"

"Georgiana specialises in giving opinions she's not qualified for," Hilda said, her top lip puckering into a slight snarl. "But, I suppose, there is a shred of truth in what she said. I used to work for the council, you see, so I know the value of the right messaging in the press. Georgiana made no secret that she wanted to be featured in the article. 'Bored Socialite Turned Volunteer' just wouldn't have the same impact, and Ronnie *is* the one who has been making the difference on the ground, bringing in cash donations and more boxes of food than we've ever seen." Hilda peeked at the shelves, which were looking even barer than when Julia had left them organised. "I just don't know how we're going to cope without—"

"*Mrs Hayward?*" A voice called through the shutters, cutting her off. "It's DI Moyes. Looks like you're finished for the day, so would you be able to accompany me to the station for some further questioning?"

"Further questioning, Detective?" Hilda called back as the shutter dragged up from the outside. "I've already told you everything I know, which amounts to very little."

"That's not quite true, is it?" She couldn't have looked more pleased with herself. Glancing at Julia, she said, "We believe you failed to report an incident of Ronnie Roberts entering your home on the very day he was poisoned."

"But I didn't—"

"Not here, Hilda. Like I said, if you'd be so kind as to accompany me to the station."

"I *shan't*." Hilda stood up, backing into the wall. "I have done nothing wrong. I know my rights."

DI Moyes clicked her fingers, and two uniformed officers appeared, going straight to Hilda as though they'd been briefed already. "Since you know your rights, I'm sure you'll understand why you're under arrest for attempting to pervert the course of justice."

While the handcuffs went around Hilda's wrists, Moyes read her the same speech that came with every arrest. Hilda's eyes searched Julia's, the same longing for help clear as when they had bonded over burnt marshmallows and again at the breakfast bar. But her expression shifted, dropping to a cold, dead stare that didn't need words to convey her feelings to Julia.

Julia could only watch as the woman who'd first welcomed her into the food bank was marched out with her hands cuffed behind her back. DI Moyes offered a semblance of an apologetic smile, but she didn't linger to explain herself.

Hilda knew it was Julia who'd let the news whisper into the wind, and she wouldn't waste her breath denying it.

9

With nobody else around to lock up, Julia loaded the trolley one last time and locked the shutters with the keys left behind on the desk. Carefully stashing the keys in the bottom of her handbag, she finished handing out the rest of the deliveries, always keeping her hands and eyes firmly on the trolley. With the police having cleared out of Ronnie's flat, Julia couldn't help but notice that the estate seemed to get busier without their blue and yellow cars littering the place. She knocked on Paige's door once more, but there was still no answer.

After driving the trolley back under the shutters, Julia made her way out of Fern Moore. She couldn't shake the hope that the police would crack the case before the end of the day so she wouldn't have to return under the same circumstances. While she wasn't convinced that Hilda was behind Ronnie's death, she knew there was always a chance she had more secrets to spill over an interview desk.

On her way back to Peridale, Julia picked up Olivia and arrived just in time to slip into the café before Sue locked up for the day. A rainbow-coloured flower arch curving around the front door and giant coconut cut-outs in the window reminded Julia of the challenge she'd set for her sister that morning, which already felt like a distant memory.

"What's that saying?" Sue grinned as she went through the takings from the till. "Necessity is the mother of invention? People loved those coconut oil cakes so much, I ran with it. Coconut carrot cake, coconut chocolate cake, coconut red velvet, coconut scones. The moment that arch went up, people couldn't stay away. It might not match Saturday's takings, but today feels like a thicker wad than our usual Mondays. Looks like you won't have to fire me and hire Gran after all."

"That was actually on the table?" Dot's voice called from the kitchen, and Sue mouthed 'washing up duty.' "And here I thought you two made a great team. Sue, take her to a tribunal if she keeps up with those threats. She'll have nothing but time on her hands now that the Ronnie Roberts case has been closed."

"The case hasn't been closed," Julia said, setting Olivia into a highchair and taking a seat herself at the nearest table to the counter. "Unless you know something I don't, they arrested Hilda for keeping secrets, and unless they find more evidence against her, she'll be a free woman by tomorrow afternoon."

"*If* they find nothing on her." Dot burst through the beads, a tea towel over her shoulder and a plate in her hands. "I always knew there was something shifty about her."

Sue and Julia exchanged amused smiles as Sue took the plate from their gran and handed it across the counter to Julia. "Some samples of my handiwork. I know you're the baking wizard in the family, but I think I'm getting better with every shift."

Julia tried each of the different coloured samples, impressed not only by Sue's baking skills with a substitute ingredient but also by how she'd turned Julia's half-serious challenge into such an event. "I would never have thought of doing all of this," she said, gesturing to the flower arch. "Where did all of this come from?"

"Believe it or not, the library. Neil had the brilliant idea of hosting a 'Tropical Tales' event to encourage kids to read over the summer holidays, and with

James Jacobson throwing money at his every idea, he's got the budget for fancy props. To think, the place was on its last legs this time last year."

"Now there's a man I do not trust," Dot declared, slapping the towel on the counter. "And I never will, no matter how much guilt money he throws at your husband, Sue. Let's not forget he was the same man who tried to turn our only public library into a restaurant."

"And let's not forget that he changed his mind," Sue replied in a quieter voice. "People aren't all good or all bad, Gran. Neil's finally getting to see the library succeed. James has kept good to his word."

"So far. And has anyone seen him since?"

Dot's question hung in the air, but with Percy waiting across the green with their two dogs, she didn't stick around long enough to push further on her 'nobody should trust James Jacobson' agenda, something that came up whenever his name did. Julia hadn't seen him since the day they'd parted outside of his new house at the bottom of her lane, and the scaffolding had still yet to be taken down to uncover what they had built there.

"I'm going to guess from the long face that your day hasn't been as good as mine?" Sue asked, settling across from Julia with a latte.

"You could say that," Julia replied with a laugh

that sounded as drained as she felt after those trolley trips up the stairs. "I'm proud of you for all of this. You know I was joking this morning?"

Sue slurped on her latte, choking on her own laugh. "Don't be daft. Of course. And Gran was pulling your leg. It's nice to have a work challenge that isn't so challenging. So, what happened today to put you in such a funk? You were bright-eyed and bushy-tailed when you left this morning."

Julia recounted her day, starting with the strange beginning at the food bank, her tour of Ronnie's flat, the food theft, and then Hilda's arrest. Sue listened intently, nodding along without interrupting.

Sue's first response when Julia finished was one of concern. "And now you somehow feel like this is your fault? First, the DI is right about the break-in being a perfect motive. And second, you did the right thing telling her. It would have come out, eventually."

"Hilda made me promise I wouldn't tell anyone, and that was after I'd already let it slip to Veronica. She came to me asking—begging—for my help, and this is how I help her? She's had an awful few days as it is, and now she's being interrogated at the station, and if they don't release her, there's a food bank down to one staff member that doesn't look like it's going to survive without Ronnie's support, and I just don't know what to do to help."

"Julia, I mean this with the best of intentions, but is this your problem?" Sue reached out and rubbed Julia's arm with her thumb. "It started off with you saying you'd help Hilda investigate a burglary, and two days later, you've got the weight of a murder investigation and the fate of a food bank on your shoulders."

"You didn't see the list, Sue. There are so many people that depend on that place." Julia bent down to pick up the cup after Olivia threw it over the side. "Families with kids."

"If I learned anything from stepping away from the hospital, it's that you need to know when to throw in the towel. You can't save everyone every time." Sue scanned the café, as though looking for a solution. "Let's focus on what we can do. How about we put out a box so people can donate food here? And a donations tin on the counter. I see people putting change into the homeless shelter pot you've had since you took Jessie in. People around here are generous when given the chance."

"It won't be enough."

"But it's a start."

Knowing her sister was right, Julia allowed herself to share in her smile. She took a sip of her comforting tea and felt some of the day's tension leave her. Sinking into the chair, she hoped Hilda wasn't having too hard a time at the station just up the road, but Sue was right about Julia doing the right thing in telling DI Moyes; she just wished the timing hadn't been so obvious.

"She looked so betrayed when she realised it was me," Julia admitted in a whisper. "I just wanted to help her, and I've made things worse."

"And what if she *is* guilty? You've just done everyone a favour by having her arrested. Things will sort themselves out."

"And if they don't?" Julia couldn't help herself. "You know, I should never have tempted fate when I told Evelyn I wanted things to stay exactly the same."

"'The universe has chosen you for a reason,'" Sue repeated Evelyn's prediction with an imitation of the same dramatic delivery, her fingers pressed to an invisible turban. "Evelyn was in here predicting the Peridale bowls team was going to win their match against Riverswick this morning, and Ethel White was in here lambasting Riverswick as a bunch of cheaters when they lost in the afternoon. If some mystic force has chosen you to solve this case or not, it doesn't mean you have to, but I know you, and I know that look in your eye. You'll figure this out. I know it." Slapping her hands on her knees, Sue stood up, prompting a giggle from Olivia, which never failed to make Julia smile. "Now, what do you say we whiz around this place, and then we take the kids to that soft play area that turns them into lunatics? Ah, we'll get it done even quicker now. You're back. Did you find them?"

The café door opened, and Jessie walked in with bags stuffed with fake flowers on the table next to them and said, "Had to go all the way to that fancy dress shop in Cheltenham, but I got what you asked for. Fifty flower necklaces."

"Why stop at the arch?" Sue winked, plucking one out and draping it over Julia's neck before doing the same for Olivia. "Evelyn's storm has come and gone, so why not make the most of the pleasant weather, eh?"

Sue busied herself stacking cups near the window while Olivia marvelled at the flowers around her neck with a smile as bright as the plastic leaves. Jessie was busy chewing her lip and watching Sue like a hawk. Sue pushed through the beads, and Jessie took the chair across from Julia. She expected Jessie would finally discuss Billy's unexpected return.

"Veronica just received a tip-off from one of her contacts at the station that they've found a car registered in Georgiana's name," Jessie confessed. "The engine was running, doors open, and her driver's license, phone, and handbag were all still on the passenger seat."

The news made Julia bolt upright in her chair. "What? Where?"

"A country lane near to here. No cameras. She's done a runner—"

"Or she's been taken," Julia finished the sentence for her. "That could explain why she went missing today."

"I heard about Hilda's arrest," Jessie said. "Apparently, she's been an absolute wreck since they took her in, and they can barely get a straight answer out of her for anything. Wasn't she the one who said Georgiana didn't turn up today and that she always turns up?"

"Yes, but what does that have to do with anything?"

"I dunno," Jessie said with a shrug. "She said the same about Ronnie too, and then he turned up dead. Could be her calling card."

"A strange calling card."

"Just spit balling." Jessie reached down to pick up Olivia's cup after she threw it to the floor for the second time. "Did Hilda say anything else about Georgiana? You said it seemed like she didn't like her much when you first told me about her."

Reluctantly, Julia said, "I got that impression today as well. She said Georgiana was some bored socialite who wanted to see her name on the front page instead of Ronnie's. Made it sound like Georgiana was volunteering out of vanity, but if Georgiana is missing, who knows what the truth is? I really wanted to talk to Georgiana, and maybe I've missed my chance."

Jessie thought for a moment before her fingers drummed on the table, launching her back to her feet. "We both know someone who might have some information about who Georgiana is as a person."

Julia wracked her brain, but she couldn't come up with anyone.

"Oh, come on," Jessie said, wiggling her fingers. "How many 'bored socialites' live around here? Let alone ones we're related to…"

10

The neon sign outside Katie's Salon was so obnoxious Jessie couldn't help but laugh at it every time she ventured down Mulberry Lane. Even on bright summer days with late-in-the-evening sunsets, the pink tubes emitted a glow so harsh to the eyes Jessie couldn't believe Peridale's oldest shopping street hadn't started a petition to have it removed.

"Jessie!" Katie Wellington-South beamed ear to ear, her cheeks looking a little fuller than the last time Jessie saw her 'step-grandmother', though the tweaks to her appearance weren't the most unusual thing about her; the fact she was the same age as Julia took that cake. "Here for an eyebrow wax? You're looking a little bushy around the edges."

"That's just how Mother Nature grows them."

"Screw Mother Nature, I say." Katie let out a girlish giggle before grabbing Jessie's hands across the counter. "Oh, dear. File and polish? I was just about to close and head off to a home appointment, but it's not like Sleeping Beauty is in any rush to wake up soon, and it looks like you need me more right now. Have you been chewing your nails?"

"Exam stress, but sure. Why not?"

Sleeping Beauty, or Brian, had his feet in a foot spa, a towel wrapped around his head, and cucumber slices on his eyes, all while snoring in a chair vibrating like a washing machine on its last spin cycle. Unlike Katie, Julia's dad was more appropriately aged to be Jessie's 'grandfather.'

"He was chasing antiques down in London for his shop all day. I keep telling him he needs to slow down, but men, eh?" Katie settled into her nail desk in the middle of the salon. "So, my new stock has just come in, and I have the prettiest iridescent shimmers, and the summer shades this year are all to die for. How about a coral? Would be a dream against your skin tone."

"How about a simple black?"

"Black it is," Katie repeated the word as though it was obscene, rolling her chair over to the wall filled with endless bottles before snatching one out. "Whatever the customer wants, right? But I suppose it'll be nice to do something simple for a change. My appointment book is filled from morning till night. Don't know whether I'm coming or going most of the time."

Jessie handed over her fingers, and Katie started shaping like she'd been doing it all her life. "But you're enjoying it?"

"Like you wouldn't believe," Katie whispered, as though it was a confession. "Who knew you could have a job and find it fun? A couple of months, and I'll have been here a whole year. Hard to remember any life before it." She stopped talking and filing for a moment as though she was remembering, but she soon continued with her usual gusto. "So, what's the goss? Any hot new guys on the scene?"

"Still single."

"Not back with that old boyfriend of yours?" she asked, wafting the file at the window. "Saw him up and down here earlier. Think he was handing out CVs. Skipped this place, but hasn't he got buff? Never thought the stringy little fella had it in him." She giggled, moving onto Jessie's other hand. "So, you're not in here to talk about work, and you're not in here to talk about boys, and you didn't come in to have your nails done, because why would you?" She squinted up at her, pointing the file right at Jessie. "That desk has fallen apart, hasn't it? I told Brian it looked wobbly when he was wrapping it, but would he listen?"

"It's not the desk," Jessie said, almost wishing she'd jumped straight to the point at the counter as Katie began adding the polish to her bare nails. "I wanted to ask you something. Or ask if you knew someone. You used to be a socialite back in the day?"

"Socialite *and* model," she corrected. "Who are you looking for?"

"Georgiana? Not too sure of a surname. She has a blonde ponytail?"

"And you thought that because I used to be a socialite years ago that I'd be able to tell you who you're looking for based on that?" Katie looked like she was trying to arch a brow, but the well-defined tail didn't lift. "I think I know *exactly* who you're talking about. It could be Georgiana Fairchild. Why, what's she done?"

"Heard about the poisoning at Fern Moore?"

"I get all the same gossip in here that you get at the café."

"She's a suspect," Jessie said, glancing at Brian as he snorted in his deep slumber. "We're trying to find out more about her, but other than knowing that she volunteers at the food bank and disliked the guy who ended up being poisoned, we're hitting dead ends."

"Volunteers at a food bank?" Katie's brow

attempted another arch as she glanced up. "Well, I suppose her dad was something of a philanthropist. Mr Fairchild ran a social welfare trust before his fortune drastically decreased. Maybe he inspired her, but last I heard, they weren't talking after her mother died. Mr Fairchild remarried some witch with a horrible son who almost bled him dry, and Georgiana went off the rails in the downfall. I know that feeling *all* too well." She dunked the brush in the polish bottle, staring through Jessie with a far-off look. "But that was a while ago, actually. Been a long time since I've been in *those* circles. I'll have to ask her when I see her. Though considering her current address, I'd guess they built the family fortune pot back up somewhat. Now *that* feeling, I don't know."

"She might have gone off the rails again," Jessie said, glad her instincts had led her to Katie. "You know where she lives? She's currently missing."

"*Missing*? Since when?"

"Anywhere between a few hours and yesterday afternoon."

"Impossible." Katie shook her head, finishing Jessie's little finger with one final swoop. "I spoke to her on the phone an hour ago."

"You *spoke* to her?"

"She's my home visit, and speaking of which, if I don't set off now, I'm going to be late. I rarely do home visits this late, and especially not *there*, of all places, but the money she offered was just too good to turn down." Glancing at the clock, Katie screwed the cap back on the bottle before clapping her hands and jolting Brian awake. "Time to pick Vinnie up, babe. I need to set off."

"Yes, my love." Brian jerked upright, the cucumbers sliding down his tanned face. "Oh, Jessie. How are things? How's the desk? Still in one piece? I picked up a smashing chair that would match. Pop down tomorrow for a look."

"Sure, I'll need to give Barker back his chair soon."

"Ten percent family discount, just for you."

"How kind," Jessie said sarcastically. "Georgiana, Katie?"

"You're off for your appointment already?" Brian blinked at the clock, unwrapping his face and using the towel to dry off his feet. "Crikey, I slept the afternoon away. Sure you don't want me to come with you? I know how you feel about that old place."

"I'll be fine," Katie said, snapping together a metal travel box. "I'm going to assume Jessie's joining me."

Waiting outside while Katie and Brian had an uncomfortably long goodbye kiss, Jessie looked up and down Mulberry Lane for any sign of Billy. He'd seemed content in the café, but it wasn't like they'd gone deep into their conversation. She still couldn't believe she'd agreed to have a drink with him.

"Thinking of moving?" Katie asked when Brian set off to his antique barn at the bottom of Mulberry Lane. "It's registered as commercial use, but I'm sure I could write to the council and ask them to change it to residential. Could see how far the old Wellington name still goes."

"I'm sorry?"

"You're staring at my sign." A long pink nail tapped against a 'BEAUTY SPACE/OFFICE TO LET,' sign stuck in the window in a ring of pink hearts. "Wouldn't it be fun to be upstairs-downstairs buddies? We'll take my car. I'm not risking you smudging those nails."

Not having the heart to tell Katie she'd been staring into space in the direction of the sign, they climbed into Katie's baby pink Fiat 500. Jessie didn't need to ask where they were heading as she tried to hide that she'd already smudged three of her nails. From the moment they set off until they were driving up the smooth driveway to Wellington Heights, once Wellington Manor, Katie repeatedly insisted that was 'absolutely fine' to go to an appointment at her ancestral home, now a luxury apartment building.

"It's not like I haven't been inside before," Katie said when they were parked outside, fingers glued to the wheel as she stared up at the enormous sandstone manor. "It's not like James Jacobson didn't give me a tour when the place was finished. Stupid building almost ruined my life. And it is just a building. Bricks and mortar."

"And memories," Jessie filled in the silence. "Katie, you don't *have* to be okay with going in there. That's also absolutely fine."

"I don't?"

"No."

"Good because I'm not." Katie exhaled, seeming relieved at the permission. "I thought I would be, but I'm really not. Not even for what she's paying me. She's in Apartment 5. I think it used to be my bedroom." Looking like she was on the verge of throwing up, Katie let go of the wheel and said, "I think I'll just wait here. Maybe you can take my kit? See how far it'll get you?"

"I don't think I'd make a very good nail technician. Not even a pretend one."

"How else will you get in? I doubt the front door is unlocked. James probably has the place covered in the best high-tech security. No expense spared, he said."

"I'll wing it," Jessie said, opening the door. "Thanks for the lift, but you should probably get home and enjoy the rest of your evening."

"Are you sure?"

"I'll be absolutely fine," Jessie said with a wink. "And thanks for the nails and the intel."

"If you want me to fix those three that you smudged and were trying to hide, swing by anytime."

Katie wasted no time reversing her car around and speeding away from the building that had almost ruined her life several times. Jessie couldn't believe anyone would want to move into the place given its cursed reputation, even before the eye-watering prices James Jacobson wanted for them. Despite the lack of 'FOR SALE' and 'TO LET' signs cluttering the front of the grand building, it was regularly gossiped about in the café that the apartments at Wellington Heights were still half empty.

Jessie approached the double front doors, a soft blue box waiting on the doorstep. She tugged at the long receipt stuck to the front, hardly able to believe she'd struck gold twice in one evening. For someone who'd been impossible to track down until her car showed up on a country lane a few hours ago, the breadcrumbs had led Jessie right to Georgiana, and the box of a dozen macarons Georgiana had ordered. Jessie scooped them up and almost pressed the buzzer for Apartment 5, but hoping her luck would continue, she gave the door a gentle push.

"Too easy," she whispered to herself as the door creaked open.

Creeping up the grand sweeping staircase wrapping around the crystal chandelier, the only part of the manor that remained unchanged, Jessie reached the landing. Apartment 5 waited for her at the end of the hall exactly where Katie and Brian's opulently gaudy bedroom had once stood. Wondering what her approach should be, Jessie cleared her throat and knocked on the door.

"Nails?" a voice called back.

"Macarons for Georgiana."

The door ripped open, and a woman in a long black robe with gold cuffs stared at her from behind a slimy white sheet face mask, her blonde hair scraped back in a painful-looking ponytail. "You took your time. I ordered these *hours* ago."

"I'll just pop them on the counter for you," Jessie said, barging in without an invitation. "Awesome place. Shame about the cracks on the walls. And is that damp?"

"That's what you get when you buy cheap." Georgiana spun around, her ponytail whipping with her. "Excuse me, that's far enough, thank you. Don't think I'll be giving you a tip."

Jessie dropped the box onto a marble kitchen island where the gigantic four-poster bed had once been. "I'm not a delivery driver. And these macarons aren't even baked well. So, how long did you think you could stay locked up in your posh apartment before someone found you?"

"I – I don't know what you're talking about," Georgiana said, a hand still on the door. "I suggest you get out before I call the—"

"Police?" Jessie plonked herself down in a cream dome-shaped chair that surprised her by swivelling. She kicked herself around once, enjoying the horror on Georgiana's face as her mask doubled over and splatted on the floor. "They've already found your car. Leaving the engine running was a nice touch. Threw into doubt if you'd legged it or just gone missing, but it turns out, neither. So, why'd you kill Ronnie Roberts?"

Georgiana's jaw flapped, but the words to defend herself didn't come.

"Ricin poisoning," Jessie said, peering out at the grounds. "Are there castor bean plants out there? Is that how you did it?"

"I didn't kill Ronnie. I didn't even know it was ricin until you said it just now."

"So, why the hiding?"

Glancing down the hallway, Georgiana half-shut the door and murmured, "Because I knew how it would look. I put my foot in it when he died."

"By not hiding how much you disliked him?"

"It's not a crime to dislike someone."

"But it *is* a crime to stage your own disappearance." Jessie pushed herself out of the chair and flipped back the lid on the box, offering it to Georgiana. She refused, so Jessie plucked one out and took a bite. "Yep, I was right. Far too chewy. So, you killed Ronnie because you were jealous of him getting that front cover?"

"I told you, *I* didn't kill Ronnie."

"It just looks that way," Jessie confirmed with a slow nod, spitting the blue mush out into the sink. "Gross. I hope you didn't pay a fortune for them, but judging by the fancy box, I'd say you did. Booking your nails and ordering macarons wasn't smart, was it? If you wanted to hide, you wouldn't be here."

"Who sent you?" she demanded, arms folding. "Was it *him*?"

Jessie waited for some elaboration that didn't come. "...him?"

"I suggest you leave right this minute."

"And go straight to the police?" Jessie pulled out her phone, and the ID badge fell out with it. Before she could pick it up, Georgiana darted in and snatched it up.

"A journalist?" Georgiana laughed. "You're just a *journalist*? Who do you think you are, barging in here?"

"A trainee journalist," Jessie corrected, attempting

to snatch the ID back, but Georgiana held it up high, the more statuesque of the two. "A temporary trainee journalist with nothing to lose and a mother with bags under her eyes after only a few days of hanging around you and your fellow volunteers."

"Oh, you're *her* daughter? I don't have to tell you anything." Georgiana yanked open the door. "Call the police. I'll be gone by the time they get here."

"Another rookie error. Why would you even admit to that?"

Georgiana's smirk dropped, and she glanced off to the side out of the corner of her eye as though wondering why she had just admitted that.

"The police are looking for you," Jessie said in a calmer voice as she headed for the door. "And they will find you as soon as I tell them where you are. Even if you run, it's only going to make things harder, especially if you're so certain you didn't kill Ronnie."

"I didn't kill Ronnie," she echoed. "I just didn't want the trouble. I thought if I kept my head down and made it look like I'd gone somewhere, I could wait things out until it all blew over. But I knew how it looked. I never liked Ronnie, and I never kept that a secret. He was a ticking time bomb. Couldn't handle his temper, and it was only a matter of time before he did something that got him and the food bank into trouble. He's never been the saint Hilda painted him out to be, but because he kept bringing in the donations, she let herself be blind to it. You know none of us knew where he *really* got all that stuff." Georgiana delivered a pleased sneer. "It was never door-to-door like he said. He'd go out, and a few hours later, he'd come back with boxes of food and fistfuls of cash. And Hilda would never ask twice, but I'd bet it was all stolen. If she'd just listened to my ideas, we could have done things *properly*."

"And what were your ideas?"

"I wanted us to throw a gala," she said, stiffening up. "Everyone gets dressed up, has a party, and the people with deep pockets donate. Raise awareness in the proper way. And if she'd let me be on the front page of the paper, I could have been a voice for them. A *proper* voice, not some urchin feeding the estate like some backward Robin Hood."

"Urchin?" Jessie couldn't hold her laugh back. "Galas? Around here? What planet are you from, or maybe I should ask, how rich are you that you're this detached? Got any evidence to back up your accusations against Ronnie's methods?"

Georgiana's jaw popped through her taut skin. "It's just obvious, isn't it? People are generous, but not that generous. There are proper ways to do things."

"Fern Moore doesn't need *proper*. It needs things that'll work, like boxes of food and fistfuls of cash."

Banana Bread and Betrayal

Georgiana's eyes narrowed to slits. "You're just like Hilda, Fern Moore's self-appointed queen. Always shooting down my ideas. Never giving me a chance to prove what I can do. You might think I'm just some dumb, rich girl living off my father's money, but I have something to offer too. But no, it's Hilda's way or the highway, but if people knew the truth about her, what she's been up to, I don't think a single person on that estate would trust her ever again."

"What's she been up to?"

"You're the journalist. *You* figure it out!" Georgiana cried, barging at Jessie with both of her hands outstretched. She stumbled backwards over the threshold and into the hallway. "You should have stayed seated. Rookie error." She tossed the ID onto Jessie's chest and slammed the door with enough force that it vibrated through Jessie's behind like she was in one of those chairs at the salon. "Call the police. See if I care anymore."

"You can count on it."

Gathering herself up off the floor with no idea why she'd chosen to be that bold, Jessie tried to go over what she'd learned from Georgiana. A lot of denial and waffle about galas, along with accusations fired at Ronnie for being a Robin Hood-type thief on behalf of the food bank, and an even vaguer claim that Hilda had 'been up to' something that would ruin her saintly reputation.

Maybe Jessie's hunch had been right about Hilda not being all she seemed after all, but she had no proof to go along with Georgiana's claims. What she had, however, was an exclusive for the paper that wouldn't stay exclusive very long.

"Scoop alert," Jessie said to Veronica over the phone as she made her way down the grand staircase two at a time. "Georgiana Fairchild is hiding out in a luxury apartment at Wellington Heights, more concerned about macarons and her nails than a man's death, and she just admitted to faking her disappearance on grounds of knowing that she looked guilty. She's packing her bags for her next great escape this very moment."

Veronica paused for so long that Jessie checked to see if the call was still connected. "I've just had to step out of the office relocation meeting with my bosses, so this better not be a prank. Because I don't know what it is about your generation and pranks, but—"

"Thanks for the vote of confidence."

"Okay, that is a scoop. Where are you?"

"I'm still at the scene of the hideout. How quickly can you get the article up? I need to tell the police."

"I'm not writing this one. *Your* scoop, Jessie." Another long pause. "Right. Here's what you're going to do. Call the police now and keep it vague, get those thumbs tapping, and make sure she doesn't flee. Let's hope we have something to publish before they figure out what you already know and release a statement. I want the first draft in ten minutes."

"Ten minutes?"

"I've seen how quickly you lot text in my lessons."

"Fair point."

"I need to get back to this meeting. They're making the right noises, so fingers crossed. A spike in traffic and paper sales would be the cherry on top right about now."

Jessie perched on the stone slab doorstep under the baking sun, and after calling the local station, she let her fingers get to work. English had been one of the three core subjects she'd struggled with the least, thanks to Johnny and Veronica pushing her so much, so she was glad when the words flowed. And it wasn't like Georgiana hadn't given her something to write about with her rambling deflections.

At the sight of the first police official, Jessie sent what she had across to Veronica, whose only reply was a 'thumbs up' emoji, which was enough for now.

"I made it, DI Moyes," a young red-faced constable panted into his radio as he slowed down his running at the top of the driveway. "Should I check this out?"

"Do *not* approach," the DI crackled. "Do you copy,

Puglisi? I'm on my way."

"Understood." He clipped the radio back to his belt before tapping on a smartwatch. "Just ran all the way from patrol near the estate. Doubled my steps for the day." Still panting, he squinted up at Jessie with a boyish smile. "You called about Georgiana? You're Barker Brown's daughter. Remember your face from the mess at the allotment."

"Apartment 5," Jessie said, not there for small talk. "Be quick. She was in a hurry to leave."

"I'm supposed to wait here." Twisting in the middle with his hands on his hips, he looked out across the rolling hills. "You know, I could always just make sure it's the same Georgiana."

"It is."

Puglisi looked up at the house and again out at the rolling hills.

"On second thoughts," Jessie said, "might be best to wait for Moyes to get here to hold your hand."

"I don't need my hand holding," he retorted with a cheeky smile, glancing at her up and down. "Not unless you're offering?"

"Dream on, pal."

His bravado vanished, his cheeks flushing red. "Maybe I'll just do a patrol of the area. See what I can find."

Jessie waited on the doorstep while the young

officer wandered around the side of the building. Almost as soon as he was out of sight, an electric car glided up the driveway, stopping in front of Jessie. DI Moyes climbed out, puffing on an electronic cigarette, which she tossed into the passenger seat before exhaling and slamming the door. She glanced over her sunglasses at Jessie, already looking irritated.

"Like mother, like daughter," the DI said. "Please tell me he didn't go—"

"Detective Inspector?" PC Puglisi sprinted around the other side of the building, out of breath again. "I think you'll want to come and see this."

DI Moyes ordered Jessie to stay where she was, but that didn't stop her from running behind the two officers to the back of the building. Hanging from Katie and Brian's former bedroom window, a line of knotted sheets flapped against the sandstone in the light breeze, signalling another great escape from Georgiana Fairchild. Given the effort she'd gone to staging her car, Jessie should have known she wouldn't try something as simple as fleeing through the front door with a suitcase.

"You have got to be kidding me!" Moyes snatched off her glasses and jabbed them in Jessie's direction. "Stay out of my case before you scare off more of my suspects, and you can pass that on to your mother, too. And not a word of this to anyone."

11

Despite not knowing if she wanted to—or even should—Julia drove to Fern Moore under a dull haze of clouds. If it wasn't for Olivia clapping out of time to the radio, Julia wasn't sure she'd find much to smile about on that Tuesday morning. By the time she reversed into the only space at the estate, light rain was pattering down on the courtyard, scattering the gathered groups. Among those rushing from the wooden play area, long red locks caught Julia's eye, as did the short purple hair belonging to Audrey. Marching to the car, she had a face like thunder to rival the grey day.

"Keys," Audrey ordered, batting her fingers into her palm as Julia wound the window down. "I'm going to assume you have them after yesterday."

"Yes, that's why I came so early, I—"

"You call *this* early?" Audrey kept her hand outstretched while Julia dug to the bottom of her handbag. "There are boxes of deliveries about to get drenched if I don't get them inside."

"I can come and help if you—"

Audrey snatched the keys and said, "Hilda called this morning from the station. Don't you think you've done enough?"

"How is she?"

"How do you think?"

With the keys in hand, Audrey ran back to the food bank's alley. Checking her list to the backdrop of the grating metal shutter being opened, Julia ticked off 'Return keys' and hovered over the second point she'd made. 'Try to talk to Paige', but Julia wasn't sure she had another rejection in her so early. She'd have taken a rainy Tuesday at the café any day, but she'd only be cluttering the place.

"What do you say, Olivia?" Julia asked, reaching into the backseat to unclip her car seat buckle. "Think we'll be as lucky as your big sister was yesterday?"

"No!" Olivia said though she delivered it with a smile.

Tugging both of their hoods on their raincoats up, Julia locked the car before sprinting across the puddles forming in the uneven concrete. She wouldn't waste her time with the lift, especially if she was about to waste her time knocking on Paige's door to be ignored again. With Olivia leading the way, Julia followed her up the stairwell to the middle of the second row. The police had moved on, leaving Ronnie's flat dark and empty.

"Mrs S? I should have known nobody else would have a car like that."

Julia spun around to a familiar voice she hadn't heard in a while. Jessie hadn't mentioned how different Billy looked, and the boy she'd hugged goodbye outside of the café over two years ago wasn't the man standing in front of her, dripping from the rain with a bag from the nearby shop. He hadn't had the lion tattoo on his neck, but that cheeky grin was still the same.

"Billy! It's great to see you. Jessie said you were back."

"Yeah?" His grin widened. "There's no way that's your kid? You'd only just found out you were pregnant when I left."

"This is Olivia. Say 'hello', Olivia."

Her greeting came out mumbled as she hid behind Julia's leg. Julia offered an apologetic smile, but Billy, as he slotted a key into the front door next to Ronnie's, said, "Unpredictable at the age, right? If she's anything like these two, you never know which version of the kid you're getting on any day."

Julia stepped back to make sure she was at the right place, but Ronnie's living room with its missing chair was still there, as was the white camera balancing on the DVDs next door. "You live here?"

"Me and Paige go way back," he said before adding, "Just kipping on the sofa 'till I can find somewhere more permanent, but even if I hadn't lost my job in the café down there, I'm not sure I could afford the new rents 'round here."

"Oh, I'm sorry to hear you lost your job, Billy. A couple of months earlier, and I might have been able to offer you something, but I've just taken my sister on."

"Seems everything has changed," he said with a shrug, the key still in the lock, door closed. "Don't worry about it. Don't think I'm suited to a café, anyway. I should have kept myself to myself, but seeing Benedict trying to force people out so soon after Ronnie died had me seeing red."

"Jessie mentioned you knew Ronnie."

Billy sent a sad smile to the flat next door. "Should have known it wasn't a coincidence that you'd be here. Mrs S is still running 'round solving mysteries. Still baking?"

"Of course."

"Then I'm glad some things never change. Don't suppose you know how to make banana bread? Had some banging stuff in the food parcel yesterday. Paige hasn't been able to stop going on about it."

"I'll give you the recipe, and I'm glad to know she enjoyed it." Julia glanced through the gap in the door as the weight of Billy's hand edged it forward, and she saw another flash of red hair. "Listen, Billy, since you're here, can you do me a favour? I'm not just here to look through Ronnie's window. I was hoping to speak with Paige. I tried yesterday, but well... she wouldn't open the door."

Billy tugged the door shut, narrowing his eyes on her. "What do you want with Paige? She's not involved."

"They were neighbours, and Hilda, who runs the food bank, said they had run-ins, and I hoped that camera might have seen something. I had a trolley full of food parcels stolen right here yesterday afternoon."

The door ripped open from the inside, and Billy jumped back from the keys. Paige took up the gap, a young baby on her hip. "And you think *I* lifted them? Who do you think you are, woman?"

"My ex that I told you about? This is her mum, and she wasn't accusing you, were you, Julia?"

"No, but I heard laughing on the other side of the door."

"Because even my Lexi," she said, jerking her head into the flat at a toddler around Olivia's age, "knows how stupid it is to leave stuff not nailed down 'round here for too long. I won't have you looking down on me, calling me some thief. I'll show you who took your food."

Paige pulled a phone from her back pocket and, after handing the baby to Billy, she tapped on the screen before tilting it sideways. She showed Julia a video of a gang of hooded lads emptying the trolley at the same speed the pigeons cleared out her bird feeders. "And I saw them down the west alley flogging them at a fiver a pop, so good luck getting them back."

"One mystery solved," Julia said, hoping a laugh would loosen the tension as the rain drilled past the open walkway, but Paige only raised a thick, drawn-in brow. "And again, I'm sorry for suggesting you might have had something to do with it, but that's not the main reason I'm here. I was hoping to talk to you about your former neighbour?"

"I ain't got nothing to say about him."

"Julia's a good egg, Paige," Billy whispered. "She's just trying to do right by Ronnie, and I know you had your feelings about him, but he was always good to me. Why don't I put the kettle on, and you can have a chat?"

Gritting her jaw as she took the baby back, Paige

looked Julia up and down, her eyes softening as she saw Olivia for the first time, who'd taken to peeping around Julia's legs.

"She about two?"

"Will be in November."

"And what are you? Must be pushing fifty?" Paige's brow drifted higher, a smile curling her glossy lips. "You her granny?"

"Paige..."

"Stick the kettle on, Bill," she said, jerking her head in. "Assumptions ain't nice, are they?"

Point made, and assuming that they were even, Julia—forty-one for a few more months—followed Paige into the small flat. They took either end of a grey sofa with more scatter cushions than Julia had seen in one place while Olivia and Lexi got acquainted over a plastic tea set. Their mothers watched on and waited in silence until Billy rushed back with two cups of tea.

"Don't have your favourite, but plain peppermint is the next best thing," he said, setting the cup next to Julia. "Julia baked the banana bread you loved yesterday, Paige."

Julia wished she'd known to bake a fresh bribery batch.

"It was fine," she said with a shrug. "Bit dry."

"Not what you said yesterday," Billy said, leaning

against the mantelpiece below the wall-mounted TV. "Why don't you show Julia that other video?"

"Because I'm no grass."

"Other video?" Julia sat upright. "Of?"

Glaring at Billy, Paige took a slurp of a milky coffee before tilting to Julia, tugging at a gold hoop in her ear. "Ronnie's brother, Norman, came 'round Friday night shouting the odds and banging on his door."

Edging forward, Julia said, "Shouting the odds about what?"

"Bunch of slurring and swearing." Paige took another slurp before leaning on her knees, placing the cup atop a tattered wedding magazine. "Norman was always coming 'round, banging on Ronnie's door, and he'd never answer. Would turn the TV up louder. Was like he'd sat on the remote or something."

"I checked out Norman's alibi at Platts Social Club last night," Billy admitted. "When he was in the café, he told Jessie he was in his flat all Friday, which he never is, but I was sure I'd seen him in there Friday afternoon. Barmaid confirmed I hadn't been seeing things, and she said had been in there Ronnie too, which he never was. Quit drinking and he must not have liked the temptation. Was in there having lunch with someone."

"Lunch with whom?" Julia asked.

"*Whom?*" Paige muttered, imitating Julia. "Hark at Lady Muck."

"She didn't see," Billy continued with a glare at Paige. "Blocked by the slot machine. Barmaid said that Ronnie looked annoyed at something, and it didn't take long for Norman to pick a fight with him. Had him pinned against the slot machine, and Ronnie didn't even retaliate, he just stood there and took it until the bouncer dragged him off."

"So, Ronnie and his brother had a fight the afternoon Ronnie was poisoned?" Julia confirmed, pulling out her pad to jot down the notes after a sip of her tea. "Don't suppose if she mentioned what he ordered. Chicken pie and mash, by any chance?"

Paige snorted. "Been the special there for about six months. Must have got a deal on a bulk of frozen pies. Or they fell off the back of a van." Teasing the wrinkled corner of the wedding magazine, she glanced at Julia out of the corner of her eye and asked, "Think that's when he was poisoned?"

"That or some cupcakes."

"Yeah?" Paige nodded. "Good. Karma works, then."

"Paige..."

"What, Bill?" On her feet, Paige walked to the door. "You think I'm going to act like that man didn't ruin my life? Ruin my kids' lives? He got what was coming to him, and you've got what you came for, Julia, so if you don't mind, I'm done thinking about Ronnie Roberts for the day."

Julia looked to Billy for another vouch, but he'd zoned out. Sensing that even pulling a fresh loaf of banana bread from thin air wouldn't change things, Julia pushed herself up and explained to Olivia that it was time to go. Both girls burst into tears at being parted so soon after becoming fast friends, leaving Julia to wish she could say the same for Paige. Once back out on the walkway, the door slammed behind Julia, only to open again.

"Paige didn't mean what she said about karma," Billy whispered, half hanging out of the door. "Her boyfriend, Josh. We were in the army together. He was a few ranks above me, but he looked out for me. Two Fern Moore lads together. And what happened to him, she blames Ronnie for his death, no matter what I say."

"I'm sorry to hear that, but why would Paige blame Ronnie for her boyfriend's death?"

"Because before Ronnie was a recovering alcoholic trying to make amends, he was a man who was proud to be in the army. He'd come 'round the estate on his leave in his uniform, and Josh looked up to him. We all did. Ronnie didn't tell Josh to sign up, but that's how Paige sees it, and with him living next door," he said, glancing back into the flat as cupboard doors slammed in the kitchen. "Just the thought of him being there alive while Josh wasn't tortured her. And I know how it sounds, but she didn't kill Ronnie. Paige doesn't have it in her. She's just grieving."

Billy ducked back into the flat, leaving Julia to stare through the window of Ronnie's flat, but in the gloom, she could only see her reflection. She'd hoped talking to Paige would clear things up, but she'd left with a stronger motive than deafening episodes of *Dad's Army*.

And then there was Norman's argument with Ronnie on the day of his death and his eventual hammering on his door when Ronnie could have already been dead inside. Had Norman known about the key under the mat? Even without being close, they were still brothers who might have shared similar quirks and special numbers. Numbers that could be used for a safe. It would lend credit to DI Moyes' theory that someone had snuck in to clear out whatever was in there.

"One more place," Julia said to Olivia after a last stab of her pen, after writing her thoughts. "Mummy has to clear a few things up."

Billy: *Drinks tonight @ 8?*

Without replying, Jessie turned her phone face down on the table nearest the window in the café. Outside, Dot and Percy hurried around the drowning green with the dogs, all four in raincoats. Jessie cleared her throat, prompting Veronica to glance up from the laptop.

"You got any exes?" Jessie asked.

Mid-bite of a slice of banana bread, Veronica gave a look that could kill. "What sort of question is that? Of course I do." Looking down at the missing bite, she added, "You made this?"

Jessie nodded. "Mum left her recipe out."

"Then you're almost as good a baker as you are a future journalist."

"You rewrote everything I sent you yesterday."

"You can learn technical writing, just like you learned to bake, but sniffing out a story?" Veronica took another bite, her eyes going down to the laptop, and through the mouthful, she continued, "You can't teach wits and guts, and you used both to beat the police to this scoop. That 'EXCLUSIVE' tag drove clicks up for the website, and app downloads were up too, and—" Fists beat down on the laptop, jolting Sue from flicking through a magazine at the counter in the quiet café, who hadn't been in the best mood without the sunshine to match her floral decorating. "I don't believe it! They were making all the right noises yesterday."

"Cotswold Media Group?"

Slapping the laptop shut, Veronica yanked her glasses off and forced herself back into the chair. "Who else? They were just smiling and nodding, humouring me to get me out of their office. All of my proposals for the local offices are still too expensive for them." Pinching the bridge of her nose, she exhaled for what felt like an age before she said, "And yes, I was married once. Why'd you ask?"

"My ex wants to go for a drink tonight."

"And do you want to?"

Jessie cast her gaze at Richie's through the rain, still closed for the morning, though a bright green umbrella with a matching tie made her sink into her chair. She dragged a laminated menu to cover her face as the bell tinkled for Benedict Langley.

"I'm looking for Barker Brown?" he called out.

"Basement," Sue called out. "Can I interest you in some coconut cake?"

"Erm, no."

"You can cut through the kitchen. I'll show you."

Jessie waited for his squeaky wet footprints to disappear behind the counter before peeking at the back of his oiled hair. He'd left his umbrella resting in the café, dripping all over the wooden floor.

"Not that it's any of my business, but if he's your ex, we're going to need to have a serious conversation."

"Get real." Jessie tossed the menu onto the laptop. "That's Benedict Langley, the guy Ronnie assaulted a fortnight ago."

"Oh, about that," Veronica said, moving right along. "I asked my contact at the station about that incident. Apparently, Ronnie had Benedict up by the collar against a wall at Fern Moore during the middle of the day. Benedict claimed there were at least a dozen witnesses, but not a single person came forward."

"Sounds like Fern Moore."

"There's more," she said, leaning closer. "Two days before Ronnie died, Benedict dropped all charges, and until then, he'd been insistent on taking the process as far as he could. With the right lawyers, the case might have gone all the way to court, but even based on Benedict's statement, it was nothing more than a shake-up."

Jessie frowned, folding her arms. She wasn't sure what, but it must have meant something.

"He left me," Veronica said, taking the last bite of the banana bread and dusting her hands. "My husband. Peter Hilt. He wanted a lovey-dovey wife who was home to put dinner on the table and baked banana bread like this, and I was too busy putting in all hours of the day into a career I didn't even care enough about."

"Can't have been much of a marriage," Jessie said, before adding, "Sorry, that was—"

"True." Veronica shrugged with a smile. "I married him because that's what you did. You got a job, met a man, married, and had kids. Got the job, met the man, and worked with enough unpleasant teenagers to never want them."

"And if he contacted you now? For a drink? Would you go?"

"Might have to go and ask Evelyn at the B&B for a Ouija board for that to happen." Her smile curdled a little as she stared down at her empty plate. "Heart disease, but he always did eat and smoke too much for my liking. I think I'd have just muddled along till the end, though. He remarried, and I didn't."

"And you kept your married name?"

"Preferred it over my maiden name, but that's a story for another day." She tucked her laptop into her bag, and after standing up, she rested a hand on Jessie's shoulder and said, "Exes are exes for a reason, but a drink wouldn't hurt anyone. I'll see what I can dig up on Benedict Langley. The police are busy running around looking for Georgiana, and they've extended their hold on Hilda, so maybe they have something concrete on her. See what you can find out about her, and we'll convene later."

"Are you free tomorrow at lunchtime?"

"I'm not third-wheeling drinks with your ex."

"Good because I'm not asking you to." Jessie twisted in her chair as Veronica yanked the door open to the heavy rain. "Meet me on Mulberry Lane for a viewing. I might be able to get a steep discount on an office."

Veronica hurried off into the rain, getting twisted up in the dog leads as Dot and Percy continued their laps, leaving Jessie to reply to the text message from Billy. Glancing at Sue back to flicking through a magazine and twiddling her flower necklace around on a finger, Jessie wondered if she could get away with putting a glass to the floor to find out what Benedict wanted with her dad.

∽

Julia hesitated outside the food bank, reluctant to face another verbal thrashing from Audrey as she unpacked the delivered boxes. The flimsy umbrella she'd purchased from the mini supermarket offered little protection against the gusts of wind threatening to turn it inside out. She waited for what felt like an eternity, her nerves on edge, until the sound of the shutters dragging down made her jump.

As Audrey locked the shutters, Julia mustered the courage to speak. "Audrey, I'm sorry about—"

"No, I'm sorry," Audrey interjected with a weary sigh. "You haven't caught me at my best. We've lost staff one after another, and now I'm all alone, with no idea if they'll release Hilda soon."

Julia tried to offer some comfort. "I'm sure she'll be out this afternoon."

Yanking up her hood, Audrey replied, "No, she won't. They've extended her hold for another twenty-four hours."

"Extended her hold?" Julia's mind raced as she grasped the implication.

"They found something in her garden. Castor bean plants."

"Ricin," Julia whispered, understanding the gravity of the situation.

"I don't want to believe it, but things aren't looking good for her."

Julia couldn't argue with that and wondered if Jessie had been right about Hilda all along. "I suppose we'll know this time tomorrow if they're going to charge her or not."

"The sooner all of this is put to bed, the better. I need to go, I'm already late for work."

"Social worker, right?"

"Yes," Audrey replied. "Back when I lived on this estate, all I wanted to do was help people, and how naïve I was. Nothing is ever straightforward. It seems the more I try to set the world right, the more things go wrong. Now, if you'll excuse—"

"You used to live here?" Julia interrupted, curiosity getting the better of her. "So, you were neighbours with Ronnie?" She hesitated, wondering if she was about to commit another social faux pas. "Listen, Hilda told me how upset you were the other night. If you know anything about Ronnie, it could help."

"I *knew* Ronnie," Audrey clarified, her tone tinged with sadness. "Past tense. We were kids, and then he left, and he returned as a different person. That's the army for you. I know nothing about Ronnie that would help in the present day. We were volunteers alongside each other, and that's it."

"But you knew him? Maybe you know who the girl in the picture was?" Julia probed further, hoping to find a clue.

Audrey glanced at her watch with a hint of irritation. "What girl? What picture?"

"He had a picture on his mantlepiece of a girl. They seemed close. It was the only picture that wasn't connected to the army, so I assumed she was someone special to him to still have it up all these years later. Seemed like a girlfriend?"

"Right. I think she moved away a long time ago," Audrey said. "And before you ask, no, I don't have a name. Look, Julia, I could stand around here all day talking about Ronnie if that's what you want, but you'll have to explain to my boss why I'm late for this very important custody case mediation."

"Then I won't keep you. I just wanted to apologise."

"I appreciate it. If you're free this Sunday, I could use an extra pair of hands." Audrey's stern demeanour softened with a rare smile. "And I could ask around about that girl in the picture and see if anyone knows where she went to pass on the message. There are still a few people from those days knocking about the place."

Promising to be there on Sunday to lend a hand, Julia stepped aside, allowing Audrey to rush off into the gloom. As she hurried back to the car with Olivia, the umbrella gave in to the wind's force, leaving Julia soaked and feeling foolish for thinking the storm had already passed.

Lingering behind the wheel and staring at the umbrella as it danced across the courtyard, Julia thought about Hilda's change of personality over their different meetings. She must have been hiding something, and with the discovery of the deadly plants in Hilda's cottage, did that mean the case was closed?

Gossip like that wouldn't stay under wraps for long, even without an official police statement. An ominous rumble of thunder reminded her that the worst was yet to come, and she didn't want to be trapped in Fern Moore to face the thick of it.

"Ready to go home and see Daddy, Olivia?" Julia asked through the rear-view mirror as the wipers struggled against the downpour. "Mummy has some deep thinking to do."

12

Jessie rushed across the green and into Richie's, her explanation for why she was ten minutes late on the tip of her tongue. She hadn't been able to send either of the cancellation text messages she'd typed out. The first version blamed the rain, the second was too honest about not being sure it was the best idea. The mental image of Billy's face dropping in disappointment at the bar had pushed her through the door.

But he wasn't there.

Only Richie and DI Laura Moyes were present. The detective was finishing a glass of something dark and brown at the bar, wincing at the final mouthful. Moyes slid the empty glass across the polished marble and put on her coat, grimacing at the sight of Jessie.

She seemed to be on the verge of saying something, but whatever it was, she thought better of it and left. Jessie still couldn't believe that her macarons stunt hadn't landed her in the same 'perverting the course of justice' trouble as Hilda.

"Looks like we're both on her bad side tonight," Richie said, placing a napkin in front of Jessie as she climbed onto a barstool beneath the row of exposed industrial bulbs. "Usual?"

"Not yet. I'm waiting for someone. Unless he's in the bathroom?"

"Hot date, is it?" Richie winked with a twinkle in his eye. "And just you, me, and—" He glanced down the bar. "My only other customer must have slipped out when the DI was grilling me. Think she might have been stood up too from the amount she was checking her phone."

Jessie shrugged off her damp denim jacket and took in the uninspired décor of the bar. The faux industrial style seemed clichéd after all the places she'd seen during her travels. For Peridale, it was the peak of sophistication and modernity.

"I haven't been stood up because it's *not* a date," she said. "Just a quiet drink with my ex."

"You're *choosing* to open the ex-file? Ouch. Is he at least cute?"

Avoiding a direct response, Jessie asked, "Why are you on Moyes' bad side?"

"Interrogating me about my dad's investments like I should know a thing about him." He rubbed the same spot on the bar in quick circles. "Haven't seen him much since he bought me this place. Should have known his promise about finally settling down after buying the manor was as true as all the other times."

Richie's father, the elusive James Jacobson, was a man that everyone in the café had an opinion of, except for Jessie; the library drama had happened during her time away.

"That's rough, mate. I'm sorry."

"That's my father for you." He glanced out the window. "And *you* might not think it's a date, but I don't think your ex is on the same page. He is cute, by the way, if not a little rough around the edges for my tastes."

Just then, Billy burst into the bar, drenched from the rain, holding a bouquet of weather-mashed carnations. His scanning gaze found Jessie, and a smile appeared on her face despite almost having called the whole thing off.

"Babe, I'm so sorry," Billy said, rushing to her with the flowers. "I almost fell off my scooter a million times getting over here. Bit wild, ain't it?"

"You rode over here on your scooter in *this* weather? Are you trying to get yourself killed?"

"I got here in one piece, didn't I?" He looked down at the bouquet. "I promise these looked better before I set off."

Jessie hadn't expected Billy to bring flowers for their 'catch-up', but it was a sweet gesture, and she accepted them with a smile. He tried to order them both pints of lager. She picked an espresso martini instead, and they paid separately. Billy joined her at the bar after suggesting they sit in a quiet corner, but Jessie felt more at ease with Richie nearby, not that she said that part out loud.

"I'm proud of you for that article," Billy said after gulping down a quarter of his pint in a few mouthfuls. "All people could talk about at the estate today. Don't think anyone liked that posh bird, to be honest. A proper condensing—" He stopped with an awkward smile as Richie placed a bowl of nibbles between them. "This place is fancy, ain't it? And check you out with your martini. The Jessie I remember used to like a can of beer on a bench with a chicken wrap from McSizzle's."

"I still like the wraps."

"Extra mayo?"

"Extra mayo." She laughed, sipping her drink; Richie made a good cocktail. "Got a taste for these when I was travelling. Kept me awake hopping all the different countries with Alfie."

"Right, the travelling. I followed along online for a bit when you first left." He paused, and Jessie couldn't help but notice a change in his demeanour. The phone calls and texts had turned into likes and comments, and then nothing. "Don't suppose he's taking on at the builder's yard? I know I was a bit crap at it, but I'll do anything right now."

"Mum told me about the café," she said, before adding, "I'm sorry, Billy. Alfie's still travelling. California, last I heard. Will be two years this New Year that we left. Twelve months, we said. I managed nine, but I think the bug got him."

"You know, I miss those days. Me, you, and Alfie. We made a good team."

Jessie missed those days too sometimes but kept that part to herself too and steered the conversation back to the safer topic of her travels. They both downed their first drinks as she entertained him with tales of their adventures across Europe, starting in Paris and heading east, ending in Tokyo when she realised all she wanted to do was come back home. Billy listened to every word, and she wondered if he appreciated not having to carry the weight of the conversation. She felt nervous, but it took his hands quite some time to stop shaking. By the time Richie replaced their drinks without them needing to ask, they seemed to relax in each other's company, and the conversation drifted to old times. They reminisced about their teenage days, which had begun when Billy was a suspect in a murder case, along with his father.

"Dad moved away too, just like my mum," Billy shared, taking the lead in the conversation as they were halfway through their second round of drinks. "At least he left a way to stay in touch. I heard from Daphne that my mum disappeared in the middle of the night with my brother and sister last year. She didn't keep in touch much once I enlisted. She ran away from debt collectors and straight into the arms of some new guy she met on the internet up in Rotherham."

"Will you go looking for them?" Jessie asked, concerned.

"Nah. They're fine. Seen them post some stuff online. It's like I never existed." Billy shifted in his seat, his expression contemplative. "I still can't believe I'm back here. When I left, I know I said I'd visit, but I thought I'd never come back."

"Want to talk about anything?" Jessie prompted. "Like why you left the army?"

"Nah." He focused on Richie as he swapped out their glasses, darting his brows at Jessie as though to say 'seems to be going well.' She took another sip, hoping she'd sleep later after so much caffeine. Drumming his fingers on the bar, Billy said, "Where were we? Oh yeah, we were talking about that time I put a brick through your mum's café window."

"And that was after you snatched her handbag from her and tried selling her phone," she said, able to laugh about it these days. "Quite the introduction."

"Things have changed. I used to be such a bad boy."

"*Used* to be? I saw you kick Benedict in the crown jewels the other day, remember?"

"And I'd do it again without a second thought." From his stern face, he meant it. "Hear about Hilda? And the poison plants in her garden?" Jessie nodded. "You asked me if I trusted her when we bumped into each other at the café, and I did. She's been sweet to everyone at Fern Moore over the years. Been helping since I was a kid, always making sure we had food after my mum spent her money on ciggies and vodka." Staring into his pint, he sighed, and said, "After your mum visited today, Paige told me something that made me think twice about Hilda."

Jessie edged forward. "What?"

"Paige and her boyfriend bought the flat off the council when he first joined the army. To give them security. She's struggling to keep up with the bills since he—" Billy choked, reaching for his pint, but he didn't lift it up. He stared out to the rain as a crack of lightning lit up the silhouette of the church across the green, and she almost told him that her mum had already shared some of the story. "Paige is doing me a favour by letting me sleep on her couch. I'm helping with the rent too. Well, I *was*."

"Something will come up," Jessie assured him. "Hilda?"

"Right." Leaning closer, he looked around the bar, still empty. "About a month before I came back from the army, Paige told Hilda she couldn't cope with the bills on her own, and Hilda started pressuring Paige to sell her flat. She made it sound like it was for Paige's own good. She almost went through with it, too, but the flat is all she has left."

"But why would Hilda want Paige to sell her flat?" Jessie wondered aloud.

"Paige thought Ronnie might have put Hilda up to it to get rid of her after all her complaining about his telly."

Jessie's mind raced with the possibilities of more motives, and a question pushed forward. "When did Benedict first turn up?"

"Around that same time, according to Paige. I'm not saying she's working with him, but it doesn't sit right with me that she'd try to get Paige to move on. Those companies that give instant cash for houses undercut market prices by twenty percent, but Benedict is giving people *half* what they're worth, and not giving them time to get other offers to even realise they're being scammed. He's making it seem like they'd never sell if they went to market. Like he's doing people favours." He snarled into his beer. "I heard a few stories in the café about people who'd sold trying to come back to find somewhere cheap to buy. The lump sum *seems* good, at first, but it's not like any bank is gonna give them mortgages to buy somewhere else. And it's nowhere near enough to outright buy these days. He's turning homeowners into renters, and ruining people's lives in the long run."

"I wonder if that's what Georgiana meant?" Jessie remembered aloud. "She said she knew stuff about Hilda that would ruin her reputation at Fern Moore if people knew what she'd been up to."

"Maybe, but I wouldn't trust *her* either. Pretty sure Georgiana was in a relationship with Benedict."

"What? How do you know that?"

"Because they were always in the café bickering like an old married couple every chance they got. Daphne barred him when she realised what the slimeball was doing. I almost bashed his head in then. Developers have been trying to get their hands on the flats there ever since Wellington Heights popped up, but he's been the worst of them. Might still have a job if I'd listened to her verbal warning about fighting. What do you think it means?"

Jessie tried to put the pieces together with everything Georgiana had said at Wellington Heights before her second vanishing act, but the martinis were fogging her mind. Instead, she said, "Georgiana said she thought Ronnie was stealing all the stuff he was donating to the food bank."

Billy snorted a bitter laugh. "Nah, that's rubbish. Ronnie was a good guy. He wasn't a thief."

"He used to steal from people when he was homeless. I knew him."

"Then you didn't know him," he said, his tone sharpening. "That was when he'd first left the army. He wasn't himself. His head wasn't right. I'd hear stories in the base about people who just gave up after being discharged. After everything they've done, everything they've seen, returning to civilian ain't easy for everyone. Hasn't been easy for me, and I didn't put in a stretch like Ronnie."

Billy was getting worked up, so Jessie let the silence rest for a moment.

"Ronnie spoke to you about that stuff?" she asked.

"A little." He shrugged. "Didn't seem to want to talk about his time in the army, but when he heard I'd dropped out, he always checked on me when our paths crossed. Could tell I was in a bad way. Didn't avoid me like everyone else." Sighing, he said, "I get it. Stuff like this is hard to talk about. I can't talk about it much, but Ronnie Roberts was a *decent* bloke. People can change, Jessie."

"That much?"

"*You* were a thief back then too," Billy said, a sudden bite to his voice. "Or have you forgotten all about how you met Julia, breaking into her café to steal cakes? Don't act like you're some angel now because you drink fancy cocktails and have your own place."

Richie stopped his bottle adjusting at the other end of the bar and shot Jessie a 'need help?' glance. She shook her head, feeling the martinis sloshing around a little too much for her liking. Billy's words stung, but they were true. She *had* met Julia that way, but she'd never pretended to be an angel. As close as they were sitting at the bar, the chasm Jessie had felt first seeing him again blasted even further open.

"Babe, I'm sorry. I—"

"My name is Jessie," she snapped, just as harshly. "And you're right. That is who I was, and Ronnie could have changed his ways just as much as I have. But somebody murdered him for a reason, and he did trespass in Hilda's cottage. I won't figure it out sitting around in here drinking cocktails and talking about old times, will I?"

They stewed, staring ahead with nothing between them but the rumble of thunder and the music. Clenching her eyes, Jessie wasn't sure how things had taken such a sharp turn and wished they could rewind back to the reminiscing.

"We're still two firecrackers, aren't we?" Billy nudged her arm with his shoulder. "I didn't mean to be so harsh. I'm just sick of people trying to paint Ronnie as something he wasn't. He kept the community fed, that's all people should remember him by. And you're right, somebody killed him, and if it was Hilda, the police already have her. And it's only a matter of time before Georgiana turns up."

"I'm sorry too," Jessie said, resisting the urge to rest her head on his shoulder. She pushed her drink away, already feeling too bold for her own liking. "Why'd you change your number, Billy?"

More silence.

"Felt like I needed to."

"But why?" Jessie pushed, almost in a whisper. "I tried to call you. Even asked around Fern Moore. I thought..."

"What?"

"Thought I'd never see you again," she admitted. "I would have stayed in touch. I wanted to. I could have been there for you after what happened to Josh." Feeling her tongue loosening too much, she added, "Sorry, my mum told me about Paige's boyfriend. That you were friends, and he died, and—"

"We called ourselves the Fern Moore Lions." He scratched at the tattoo on his neck. "He was a Lance Corporal when I was in basic training. Not supposed to be mates through the ranks like that, but he recognised me straight away. Looked out for me. Those first few weeks were tough." He glanced at her, but his eyes didn't quite meet hers. "Told me it was normal to be homesick, but I kept putting my foot in it with my big mouth. They kept punishing me for the dumbest stuff. I couldn't handle it. Josh said I was like a baby lion, roaring at everything and everyone because I was scared, and he was right." Sniffing hard, his eyes locked on Jessie's. "It was a landmine."

"Oh, Billy..."

"South Sudan," he continued. "He'd been chosen for a 'routine stabilisation mission', and that was the last thing he said to me. They were supposed to have swept the area, but it only takes one. They said he was out on patrol, and that it would have been quick. Wouldn't have even known it was happening, but do you think that helps Paige sleep at night?" Clenching his eyes, Jessie held out her napkin from under her drink, but he didn't take it. "He still owes me a *Call of*

Duty rematch. They were supposed to be getting married in the New Year."

Jessie didn't know what to do or say, so she clenched his hand, and he wrapped his fingers around hers, clinging tighter than he ever had. They sat in silence again, this time a little less uncomfortable.

In a small voice, Billy said, "Before I left, I said I was going off to find out who Billy was without Jessie. I don't think I found him." Letting go of her hand, he patted it. "When I got back, I wanted to come and see you straight away."

"You should have."

"I went to your café." He glanced at the rain with a sad smile. "Didn't even get through the door. You had your head in some book, and Julia was behind the counter like nothing had changed. Your gran and that nutty woman from the B&B were going back and forth, and one of them said something that made you all laugh. Just seeing you so happy, I went back to the estate and swore I'd leave you alone."

"You *should* have come in," she restated, holding back tears of her own. "You were the best friend I'd ever had, Billy, and then you were gone."

"We made pretty good pals, didn't we?" His cheeky smile broke out, and she gave in to the urge to rest her head on his shoulder. "I know there's no going back, but I just miss having you in my life, Jessie." They stayed there for a moment before Billy laughed and said, "Listen to us. When did we get so old?"

"We have a lot of history. We're always going to have a bond."

"Yeah, we are, aren't we?" He sniffed and took the napkin he'd refused the first time. "So, what do you say? Think we can be friends?"

"I hope so."

Approaching from the other side of the bar, Richie cleared his throat.

"Not to eavesdrop, but it's as dead as a doornail in here," he said, plucking out a bottle. "I wouldn't be doing my duty as a bartender extraordinaire if I didn't propose a toast." He poured himself a shot of gold tequila and raised it high. "To new beginnings?"

"New beginnings," Billy lifted his glass.

Jessie clinked her martini glass with Richie's shot. She did the same with Billy's pint, and the stem shattered on impact. The glass slipped from her grip, soaking her white t-shirt. Through her laughter, she said, "To new beginnings."

"I could kill my father." Richie snatched up a towel and started wiping down the bar. "For all his money, he's one hell of a cheapskate. I'll pay for a replacement shirt."

"Got it from the charity shop. Don't worry about it. I'll be right back."

Jessie excused herself to the bathroom, her emotions swirling inside her like the storm outside. As she stood before the bathroom mirror, her heart sank at the sight of the giant dark wet patch clinging to her stomach. Taking a deep breath, she tried to process everything that had just happened.

Billy had been through so much, and hearing him talk about losing his friend broke her heart. She'd meant it when she mentioned the bond they shared. Even after years apart, with so much water under their bridges, she could still feel the connection to his pain. She wished she could do more to help him heal. A part of her had always held on to the hope that they'd find their way back to each other someday.

She wouldn't have tried to call him otherwise.

But they were on different paths now.

Leaning over the cold marble sink, she rubbed the fabric under the water rushing from the ornate brass tap, trying to calm her racing thoughts.

Friendship *was* the best outcome for them.

Despite the memories of what might have been, she was the one who had put an end to their romance. She'd been on the verge of nineteen, eager to move into her very own flat above the post office, and Billy had wanted to move in with her, talking nonstop about weddings and kids. He wanted it all, and he'd been in a rush. Breaking Billy's heart had never been her plan, but she couldn't force herself to want the same things he did. Twenty-one, and she still didn't see that kind of future. After her upbringing, would she ever?

Shaking her head to bring herself back to the present and remembering why she had stopped drinking during the second half of her travels, she looked down at her shirt. The stubborn stain refused to budge, and the cheap fabric had soaked through up to her collar. With a defeated sigh, she knew it was time to go home. She stepped away from the counter and searched for the hand dryer, noticing a pair of white trainer soles sticking out from under a stall.

"Bit early for throwing up, isn't it?" she called out, trying to bring back the lightness she'd felt before the toast. "You holding up in there?"

There was no response.

Looking back over the night, Jessie tried to recall if she'd heard the door open as the storm had raged outside. She'd been in a bubble with Billy, but even Richie had just pointed out that they were alone. No one else had come in from the rain since Billy, and that had to have been at least a few hours ago.

The realisation sent a chill down her spine.

"Hello?" Jessie called out again.

With the tap still running, Jessie turned around, her wet t-shirt dripping on the tiles as she tried to blink away the blurriness. Maybe she was imagining things? But she was only tipsy, and those shoes hadn't moved an inch. Taking a deep breath in the uneasy silence, Jessie walked closer to the stall, her hand outstretched.

13

In the nursery at the cottage up the lane, Julia saved her page in *The Wonderful Wizard of Oz* with her finger, sharing in Barker's sleepy smile. Lost in the story, she hadn't noticed how long he'd been leaning against the doorframe, wearing the navy pyjamas she gifted him last Christmas.

"Don't stop on my account," Barker whispered, tiptoeing across the room. Standing behind her, he rubbed her shoulders with a magic touch that made her head roll back. "I want to find out what happens when Dorothy gets to the Emerald City."

Julia tossed the book on the table with the nightlight. "To be continued. Olivia fell asleep long ago, but I needed to take my mind off things. Did you get many pages written?"

"Enough."

Resting her head on his stomach, she peered up at him as he examined the stars on the ceiling, though he didn't seem focused. "Something on your mind?"

"You know me too well. I met with Benedict Langley today."

Julia twisted in the rocking chair, and Barker backed away, leaning against the wardrobe. "What kind of meeting?"

"The private investigator kind, and it wasn't the first."

Confused, she said, "You kept that quiet."

"Benedict tried to hire me about six weeks ago," he explained, pulling his reading glasses off and rubbing his tired eyes. "Amazing what glasses can do for a man's appearance. He had a full beard too when he came to my office the first time. He scrubs up well. Never would have recognised him seeing him at Fern Moore on Sunday, but Jessie told me his name and it's been bugging me ever since, so I went digging through my paperwork."

Julia wasn't sure what it meant, but she was all ears. "Sounds like he was in a bad way?"

"By his own admission, he was broke. Claimed he was about to come into some 'big money,' and I'd get paid in a few months if I helped him. I'd only just started getting serious about my writing again, so I declined. It seemed like he wanted a bodyguard more than a PI."

"A bodyguard for what? And how did he go from being broke to snapping up flats all over Fern Moore?"

"Well, that's why I invited him to my office today, to find out. Thankfully, he didn't recognise me from Sunday either, but he must hand out tons of those flyers every day. I told him I'd been reconsidering his case, and he said he no longer required my services, so I got to the point and asked him if the reason had anything to do with the recent death at Fern Moore."

"And?"

"I played a little dumb," he said, slipping his glasses into the top pocket of his pyjama shirt. "Flattered his business prowess after he bragged about 'turning his misfortunes around.' He told me it had something to do with Ronnie, not that he used his name at that point. Kept things vague like he did during our first encounter. He said he had some 'opposition from the locals' to his development plans, and that's why he wanted to hire me. He didn't *explicitly* say it, but I think the implication was that he wanted me to dig up dirt on anyone who stood in his way, to discredit them."

"Benedict wanted you to discredit Ronnie?" Julia echoed, staring into a dark corner of the nursery. "I suppose it makes sense for Ronnie to be against whatever he's doing at Fern Moore. He cared enough about the place to put in the hours he did."

"And Benedict was doing his fair share of discrediting."

"How so?"

"He mirrored what Georgiana said about Ronnie stealing supplies and claimed that the police 'had the right person in custody.' He didn't know about the ricin plants being found in Hilda's garden though, and Moyes wasn't too happy to find out we knew either. I mentioned the assault and him dropping the charges, and he said he did that as a 'gesture of goodwill to the community,' but he dodged any mention of why Ronnie had him up against a wall."

"So much for him telling Jessie he didn't know who Ronnie was."

Barker walked over to the window to stare out at the blackness of the storm, the only nearby lights being the glow from Veronica's cottage. "But I brought up that he could be a suspect, which didn't seem to faze him. He said the police have already talked to him and confirmed his alibi."

"Must be a good one if it's ruled him out?"

"He was in Oxford for a charity gala all Friday, and Moyes confirmed that witness statements put him at the estate every day *except* for Friday. He checked into *The Randolph Hotel* Thursday afternoon and checked out Saturday morning, by which point, Ronnie had already been poisoned and was presumably dead."

"Waiting for Hilda and me to find him on Sunday afternoon."

"There's something else too." He reached into his top pocket and pulled out a small green book before slipping his glasses back on. "My client chair is nowhere to be found, so I had to sit him on the Chesterfield, and his suit material kept slipping against the leather. Must have slid out of his pocket from all the fidgeting. I almost missed it poking out of the side of the sofa."

"What is it?"

"Benedict's diary."

Leaving the rocking chair, Julia joined Barker at the window.

"You've read his diary?"

"Don't worry, it's not filled with his darkest desires and wildest dreams." He flipped through the blank pages. "Appointments, reminders, that sort of thing." He paused on one page that had a to-do list with 'Buy milk, suit fitting, check on Mum,' all ticked off. "Nothing of note in here, except for one little mystery."

"Like we don't have enough of those right now."

They shared a smile, and he said, "Three appointments in the week leading up to Ronnie's death, all ticked off. The last one was on Thursday morning before he left for *The Randolph*. Looked it up online, and it's a classy place, by the way." Flipping forward a few pages, he tapped on a square and read, "'Meeting with LB.' Does LB mean anything to you? I presume they're initials?"

"LB?" Julia repeated aloud, shaking her head. "Doesn't ring any bells. Do you think it could mean something?"

"I'm not sure, but I'll keep digging." He slotted the book back into his pocket, and added, "Right after I get this back to him, of course."

"Of course."

"So, what do you say we get to bed, and—" Barker squinted into the darkness, cupping his hands against the glass. "Not *again*. There's someone coming up the garden path."

For the second time that week, a fearful face appeared at Olivia's nursery window. Though it wasn't a grandma from a storybook, it looked more like a witch, and it was Jessie. Her hair plastered to her head and eyeliner speckled down her cheeks, Julia's mind went straight to the catch-up drinks.

"Put the kettle on," she whispered to Barker. "I've got this one."

"And here I thought we were long past the Billy heartbreak days."

At the front door, Julia wrapped her soaked daughter in a hug. Despite the night air being muggy, Jessie shivered, and Julia could only imagine how bad things had gone. Based on Billy's smile when she'd brought up Jessie at the estate earlier that day, Julia hadn't been feeling too optimistic that the drinks at Richie's would take the casual route Jessie had hoped for.

"Do you want to talk about it?" Julia whispered as Barker filled the kettle at the kitchen sink, but Jessie said nothing as she pulled back from Julia's hold. "There's still that bag of your old clothes in the airing cupboard. Why do you smell like coffee?"

"E-espresso martini," Jessie stammered, her jaw moving like it didn't belong to her. Her mouth curled down into a look so pained Julia's gut twisted into immediate knots. "I found Georgiana again, Mum." Tears streamed down her cheeks, disrupting the eyeliner blotches in fresh rivers. "She's dead."

14

The coarse fabric of the old duvet scratched against Jessie's neck, but it couldn't distract her mind from revisiting the scene she'd stumbled upon in Richie's bathroom. Her heart pounded in her chest, fuelled by adrenaline and late-night espresso.

Twisting in the duvet, she couldn't shake the haunting images.

Georgiana had been in there dying while she was sipping cocktails and reminiscing about the past. Her pasty face had been so pale it blended into her blonde hair, her limp body slumped over the toilet as if she had taken a mid-hurling nap. Why had Jessie needed to look over the top of the stall when she should have just called for help?

Billy's silent shock had mirrored her own when

they'd held each other before the police separated them for statements. She longed for the familiar grasp of his hand, wondering where he was now.

"I thought she'd left," Richie had kept repeating. "I really thought she'd left."

Jessie bolted upright in the dark, drawing in a sharp breath. She searched the sitting room of the cottage. Spotting Julia in the armchair, lost in her notepad, Jessie's panic eased a little. Her mum was there, working on the case.

Julia was cracking it.

She had to be.

Not wanting to disturb her notetaking, Jessie tucked herself back under the duvet, facing the back of the sofa. The torment persisted, and a fresh feeling washed over her—guilt.

If she hadn't barged into Georgiana's apartment, if she hadn't written that damning article, perhaps Georgiana would still be alive.

Maybe the police would have found her, maybe she would have ridden out the storm with her face masks and macarons until they caught the actual murderer.

Jessie squeezed her eyes shut, wanting to force away the feeling, but it clung to her like the restless caffeine in her bloodstream.

She was sure she'd never sleep again.

Julia stirred as a gentle hand shook her shoulder, finding herself still upright in the armchair. Soft morning light seeped through the thin curtains. The storm had subsided, leaving dawn to be welcomed in by chirping birdsong. From his dishevelled hair, Barker had just woken.

"You should come to bed," he suggested, brushing her matted curls away from her face. "It's just gone five."

Rubbing the sleep from her eyes, she couldn't recall when Jessie's restless tossing and turning had given way to peaceful snores, but that was when Julia had allowed her own heavy eyelids to close. She pulled herself upright a little, the grog of only a few hours turning her into a lead weight.

Barker picked up her notepad from the floor. "Made any progress?"

A weary sigh escaped her. "I have some ideas, but I keep going over the same things." She recounted Jessie's revelation about the possibility of Georgiana and Benedict being lovers, then added, "Benedict might have killed Ronnie for the reasons you said, and she found out, and this was his revenge."

"He has that alibi," Barker reminded her, a note of caution in his voice. "It can wait until morning, love."

He draped a blanket over her and leaned in to give her a kiss. "Get a few more hours of rest, and maybe keep the café closed tomorrow?"

"I'll think about it." Julia would be opening in a few hours. There was no turning back now, and she'd have a front-row seat to the latest crime scene. Mowgli hopped onto her lap, and with the same purring determination of him kneading the blanket, she said, "I'm going to solve this case one way or another. For Jessie's sake. And Georgiana's. And Ronnie's."

15

*J*ulia cherished the mornings when her family gathered at the cottage, but she couldn't help but wish they were there under better circumstances. Despite the situation, they appeared content and joyful as they sat together in the kitchen on a textbook summer morning. Jessie, though obviously exhausted, made an effort to keep things light, possibly for Olivia's sake; she was the only one who seemed to have had a restful night's sleep.

"Bacon sandwich for madame," Barker announced as he placed a plate in front of Jessie at the breakfast bar. "Extra ketchup, just the way you like it. And for the other madame, a strong coffee." Julia expressed her gratitude with a smile as the steaming cup replaced her untouched porridge. "And for little madame, how about another slice of toast?"

"Toast," Olivia repeated, though it came out sounding more like 'toads.'

"Stick me a slice in too," Jessie said. "I need to feed this hangover."

As Julia took her first sip, she gathered the courage to ask, "How are you feeling?"

"I've felt better," Jessie replied, wiping ketchup from her lips and hunching over her plate. "I'll feel better when we know what happened to Georgiana. We can rule out Hilda since she's been under lock and key for the last few days."

Julia had made a similar note, hoping the police had reached the same conclusion and released Hilda.

"That's if the same person poisoned both of them," Barker added. "But I think you're right. I never thought it was her, to be honest. Hilda was the one seeking the truth."

"We still don't know what Ronnie took from her," Julia said, referring to her earlier notes. "But I hope I'll be able to talk to her at some point today. Who knows, she might be waiting on the café doorstep right now."

Glancing over his shoulder as he buttered the toast, Barker asked, "You're opening the café?"

"I am."

"I'll come and help," Jessie offered.

"You should stay here and catch up on your sleep."

Jessie finished her sandwich and, without waiting to swallow, took a bite of the fresh toast Barker had just added to her plate. Through the mouthful, she said, "How am I supposed to sit around and do nothing when all of this is going on?"

"Your mum is right," Barker said. "I'm thinking of heading over to *The Randolph* to double-check Benedict's alibi. Oxford is only an hour away, so there's a chance he could have slipped in and out at some point."

"Then I'll go to Fern Moore," Jessie said. "I want to talk to Norman again. He hates his brother, so I'm not ruling him out yet. There might be a reason he hates Georgiana, too."

"Rest," Julia insisted after another sip. "I can talk to Norman. I want to see if I can catch Audrey at Fern Moore at some point. I still feel like she's holding something back about Ronnie."

"I read your notes while you were in the shower," Jessie said, "and from what you've written, it looks like she disliked Ronnie being at the food bank as much as Georgiana did. She just wasn't dumb enough to keep saying it. And then there's Paige. Billy is convinced she has nothing to do with it, but every time he tries to defend her, it adds another motive."

Julia couldn't disagree. As weak as the motive of being fed up with his TV might seem, blaming him for her late boyfriend's army enlistment and the subsequent landmine incident was one of the strongest motives among the suspects. But like with Hilda, Julia didn't want to believe it.

"I want to understand why Hilda would want Paige to sell her flat," Julia said as she slid off the stool and picked up Olivia from her highchair. "Dad's watching her today, so I'll be at the café until closing if anything happens before then. Jessie, please try to get some more sleep." Julia kissed her on the top of the head. "And maybe have a shower. Barker, let me know if you find out anything in Oxford. It would be great if we could put an end to this today."

After getting dressed and glad to see Jessie crawling back under the duvet, Julia left the cottage with Olivia. She dropped Olivia off at her dad's cottage and headed to the café. Hilda wasn't waiting for her on the doorstep as she had hoped, but the lights were already on inside.

Despite not being scheduled, Sue was waiting for Julia with an island full of baking supplies. After taking down the flower arch, which they both agreed was in poor taste given the forensic officers heading in and out of the white tent erected in front of Richie's, they prepared for the inevitable morning rush.

"You don't have to stay," Julia said when the ovens were full. "I've just had two days off. Consider me rested enough to deal with whatever today throws at me."

Sue smiled, dusting flour off Julia's cheek. "You might not want to lie to medical professionals about being rested with dark circles like those, big sister. I don't mind sticking around."

"You're spending the day with your twins," Julia insisted, pulling the apron over her sister's head. "Employer's orders."

Sue left through the back door, and the icing and decorating kept Julia distracted enough until opening time. After filling the display cabinets and flicking on the music, Julia assured herself a day alone in the café was nothing she hadn't done hundreds of times before.

Flipping the sign on the front door, she stared across the green to the bar, where the morning dog walkers were already congregating to watch the investigation unfold. Among those hanging around on the pavement, DI Moyes caught her eye, and they exchanged a nod. A subtle acknowledgement of their shared determination to unravel the truth, perhaps? A far cry from the message she'd give Jessie to pass on to her about staying out of the case. As Julia was about to flip the sign back and cross the green to approach the detective, Evelyn swept into the café in a swathe of mourning black.

"I *knew* it!" she declared. "I *sensed* something terrible would happen during the storm."

Julia furrowed her brow, trying to recall Evelyn's earlier prediction. "Did you mention that part?"

Evelyn paused, accessing the depths of her mystical memory. "Perhaps not *vocally*, but I *felt* it."

Under normal circumstances, Julia might have chuckled, but she thought back to the skull in the teacup. Another day, another body, and from the grim expression on DI Moyes' face as she approached the café while Evelyn took her usual table, the case was no nearer being closed. Moyes stepped inside and followed Julia back to the counter, where she started on Evelyn's regular pot of tea. She'd let it steep behind the counter and take the teabags out herself this time.

"Quite the night," Moyes said with a tight smile. "Julia, listen, I need to apologise for the way I spoke to Jessie at Wellington Heights. It was uncalled for. Tensions are high at the station right now, and she's young, and finding a body like that must've been hard on her. How's she holding up?"

"She'll be fine," Julia said, keeping it short. "I'll pass your apology on. I think we all want the same thing."

"That we can agree on."

"Coffee?" Julia twisted the arm of the bean grinder. "How's Richie doing?"

"We spent the night questioning him," she said, leaning against the counter to stuff her hands into her hair, and Julia assumed Moyes had been the one hurling questions at him all night. "Richie insisted that Georgiana barely touched her drink. He seems more shocked than guilty, and we have no reason to suspect him, even if they were neighbours at the manor. He seems to live in his own bubble up in that penthouse. Hadn't even heard she was a murder suspect, let alone that she was on the run. I dodged a bullet by not buying one of those apartments. People around here say that manor place is cursed."

"I don't believe in curses," Julia said, glancing at Evelyn, who opened a clenched eye from her meditative state. "So, you've released him?"

"A free man as of an hour ago."

"Then make sure that's clear to everyone. Richie doesn't need his reputation ruined by poisoning rumours." She frothed up the milk and added, "I assume it was poisoning again?"

Moyes nodded, eyeing up the banana bread—with walnuts, this time—twirling around under the spotlights. "Ricin, again. We believe she ingested the poison earlier in the day. Richie said Georgiana appeared agitated from the moment she arrived.

Checking her phone, looking at the door. Any idea who she might have been expecting?"

Julia thought for a moment, her mind returning to Jessie's confessions when she'd sat down after coming in from the rain. "Benedict, perhaps? They were seen at Daphne's Café in Fern Moore. Bickering like an old married couple, apparently."

"What is it with *that* place and keeping secrets?" Moyes huffed, tapping the detail out on her phone. "I get not wanting to 'grass on your own,' but with everything going on? I'll look into it *if* I can get anyone to talk."

"Benedict has that alibi."

Moyes looked at her, surprised. "And what is it about *you* knowing things *you* shouldn't? And on second thoughts, how did you know about the—"

The café door banged open, jolting Evelyn from her meditation. Dot lugged in a crate full of cereal boxes and dumped it on the first table. Percy trailed behind her, struggling to drag a cart full of rattling tins over the threshold. Julia pressed the lid on the takeaway cup and slid it across with a paper bag of banana bread without the DI needing to ask. Julia didn't put it through the till; she'd probably skipped breakfast. Moyes tapped her phone on the contactless payment portal for the coffee and excused herself with a toast of the cup.

"Sue told us all about how worried you were the other day about the food bank not getting enough donations," Dot announced as Percy began unloading their donations onto a vacant table. "We rallied Shilpa and Amy yesterday before the worst of the storm and gathered all of this from across Peridale. *This* one," Dot said, nodding at Evelyn, "was too busy 'charging her crystals.'"

"Full moons are *very* important," Evelyn remarked as Julia set the pot of tea in front of her. "Did you know there was once a cult dedicated to worshipping the moon right here in our—"

"How interesting," Dot interrupted, squinting at a box's label. "Typical. This one is pushing the use-by date. Percy, make a note that the cornflakes need to be given out first."

"Right, you are, my dear. Joining us today, Evelyn? We're hitting Riverswick." Percy rubbed his hands together before patting down for something to make a note. "They've got more money knocking about the place."

"You can count me in."

"Extra pair of hands means more houses," Percy said, "and every little helps."

"This is far from little," Julia said, pulling them both into a hug. "This food is going to make a difference. I'll take all of this across later." Outside, a group of women approached the café from the direction of the church, curiosity gleaming in their eyes, their tongues no doubt wagging behind their dentures, ready to gossip the morning away. "And so, it begins."

"You do your thing," Dot said, patting Julia's cheek. "Let your gran do what she does best."

As one woman shouted a question at the lingering police officers about updates, Dot emerged from the café and called, "Ladies, I have *all* the details! You're never going to believe this, but it was *my* great-granddaughter who found her sticking out of the toilet like someone tried to flush her away!"

Julia almost corrected her gran, but there was no point. The story would be something else by noon, and another thing before closing. She retreated behind the counter and pulled out her pad to go over her notes again.

Whatever happened, the day was sure to be a long one.

16

Dragging herself off the sofa for the second time that morning, Jessie threw herself into the shower before driving to Mulberry Lane. With everything that had happened, she'd forgotten all about the offer to show Veronica an office until the editor's text message reminder. She drove around the fallen branches being cleared away from the cobbled road by the locals, but even with the blinding morning sun, Jessie knew she couldn't clear away her own storm mess so easily. She spotted Veronica checking her watch outside the wedding dress shop and parked.

Veronica greeted Jessie as she climbed out of the car. "I don't see any 'TO LET' signs. You promised me an office viewing."

Jessie pointed across the road to the ever-present pink glow of Katie's Nails, and then the empty window beneath the new roof, one of the few that wasn't sagging on the old row. Maybe Jessie was imagining it, but the colour seemed to drain from Veronica's face.

"I'm not sure this is what *The Peridale Post* is looking for. It's a little *pink*."

"You're looking for cheap, aren't you?" Jessie backed into the road, jerking her head for the editor to follow. "Recently renovated, no corners cut. Was a bookshop before it burned down. Beats a leaky roof in an old office block, doesn't it?"

Veronica's lips parted, but the protest that was itching to burst out didn't come. Fiddling with her enormous frames—black today, though the subdued colour didn't make them look any less whacky—she followed Jessie across the road as Katie yanked open the door from the inside.

"Isn't this exciting?" Katie squealed, gripping Jessie's arm. "The newspaper above *my* salon!"

"You sound like an avid reader?" Veronica asked.

"Oh, no." Katie shook her peroxide curls. "It's just through here. Watch out for Vinnie. He's been bouncing off the walls all morning."

Veronica looked queasy as she danced around three-year-old Vinnie, zooming around the salon with his arms spread out like an aeroplane, and making the noise with buzzing lips to match. Veronica shook her head at Jessie, but Jessie followed Katie up the narrow staircase to the spare rooms above the salon.

"Five hundred a month," Katie explained, opening the door to the white, empty room. "And that includes Wi-Fi, water, and electricity. If you have questions, I'll be downstairs, though I might be awhile." She leaned in and whispered, "I have Mrs Coggles in for a moustache wax, and she's *very* particular."

Once alone, Veronica walked around the space as though she'd just learned to walk for the first time. She peered out of the window with the caution of someone approaching an active bomb, the pink glow gleaming against the glass.

"Enough room for four desks, I'd say. Maybe even a small kitchen area too," Jessie said, pulling open a door. "There's even a bathroom."

The two of them stared into the small room—more a cupboard—with the tiny toilet and sink. Jessie saw Georgiana and slammed the door shut.

"It's a little small," Veronica said, hands deep in her pockets as she took in the room. "Price seems too good to be true, too. Couldn't find anything below a thousand. What's the catch, and how do you know her?"

"No catch, and there's a separate fire escape

entrance at the back," Jessie added, dodging the question. "Wouldn't have to go through the salon. Could even get a little sign."

"Maybe Katie is the catch. Something tells me she won't be easy to avoid every day," Veronica whispered, craning her neck around the door to the staircase. "How are you feeling after last night, anyway?"

"I'm fine," Jessie replied, folding her arms, her turn to stare out of the window. The last branch was being thrown into the back of a van like nothing had happened at all. "Can't shake the feeling it might not have happened if I hadn't gone in all guns blazing."

"What happened to Georgiana could have been set in motion before your article. Don't blame yourself, Jessie. You conducted a fine piece of investigative journalism, which is what this paper needs."

Jessie nodded as Veronica's hand weighed down on her shoulder. She still wasn't convinced she'd done the right thing, but Veronica wouldn't say otherwise. She'd got her website clicks and app downloads. Deciding to change the topic, she asked, "You said you were going to dig into Benedict. Find anything?"

Veronica's expression turned serious as the two of them sat on the top step of the metal fire escape. There was a small courtyard like the one behind the café, along with a view of the back wall of a long-abandoned cotton mill.

"I started digging in my Greg Morgan folder," Veronica said. "And let me tell you, I was surprised that his name didn't come up anywhere in connection to our local Member of Parliament. Every dodgy name around here seems to lead back to Greg."

"But not Benedict?"

Veronica shook her head, and she glanced at Jessie as though saying, 'I know Johnny gave you a copy of the folder too,' but she didn't push the topic.

"So, I broadened my search and stumbled upon some old articles from the *Cornish Guardian*," she revealed. "Turns out, Benedict's mother married into *old* money, and our friend Mr Langley got his grubby hands on a chunk. Tried his luck investing in the holiday letting business along the south coast, which would have been a foolproof investment for anyone."

"Don't tell me," Jessie said. "It wasn't foolproof for him?"

"No, and the man does seem like a *fool*. Royally mismanaged his portfolio, renting out places he'd let fall into total disrepair. Cracked walls, unsafe roofs, mould of every colour, water-filled basements. You name it, the list goes on. Some people got seriously hurt. People fell ill. One woman breathed in so much black mould without realising it, she was hospitalised for a fortnight."

"I'd sue."

Veronica gave a triumphant smile. "They did, and they bankrupted him. He had to sell the lot and flee Cornwall for the Cotswolds."

"So, how did he end up in Fern Moore, of all places?" Jessie thought aloud. "And how is he affording to buy flats at the rate he is?"

She shrugged. "Rich people know other rich people. He must have found some willing investors to back him. Could have promised them profits beyond their wildest dreams, but he's left all the flats he's gained empty. Hasn't even started modernising them."

"Maybe he's out of his depth?"

The floorboards creaked behind them, and they turned to see Katie emerge at the top of the stairs. "Only me," she announced, wiping her forehead with the back of her hand. "Mrs Coggles is now moustache-free. So, what do you think?"

Standing up, Veronica considered the space, and with a sigh, said, "I'll have to crunch the numbers and convince the bigwigs, but this could be a viable option. Having our headquarters so central *would* be a big bonus."

"How exciting!" Katie grinned. "We're going to be upstairs-downstairs neighbours. And you can have any treatments you want whenever I'm free, on the house. I could even sort out your..." Katie's finger motioned in the space between Veronica's eyebrows. "My clients will never believe this. Me, having a salon right under *The Peridale Post*. Might have to start reading it."

Veronica held in whatever she wanted to say, even when they were alone on the pavement outside, using the window to look at whatever Katie had seen. "Do I have a unibrow?"

"If you did, those glasses cover it up. She's harmless. Her hot wax and threading string, I'd stay away from."

Peering up at the gleaming sign, Veronica looked a little less sickly than on the way in. "How did you say you know her again?"

"I didn't," Jessie said, suppressing a smile. "Katie Wellington-South is my step-grandmother, and that toddler terror knocking polishes off the shelves is *technically* my uncle."

"You're not joking, are you? Wellington as in Wellington Heights?"

"The same, and it's a long story."

"And I thought my family was complicated." Veronica walked backwards into the road towards Jessie's Mini. "You can fill me in on the way. Lunch at Daphne's, on me. And who knows, we might just bump into bankrupt Benedict to see what he has to say for himself. There's still time to dig up a scoop before the next issue goes to print."

~

In the café's kitchen, Julia mixed the scone dough, her hands moving with practised efficiency. The aroma of the batch fresh out of the oven filled the air, making her stomach grumble. She glanced at the clock on the wall, noticing the morning had bled past noon. The crime scene rush had kept her more than occupied, and it showed no signs of slowing.

Her gran had kept good to her word, entertaining the full house with the titbits she knew. Julia had declined her request to read through her notes, so Dot had been left to fill in the blanks with her usual creative flair. It had left Julia to focus on keeping the ship steady on the waves of the latest poisoning, and until the police left Richie's, she still had the best seats in the village.

With the next scone batch baking in the oven, Julia took the stool at the counter and crammed in a ham and cheese sandwich. Pen primed over the notepad, she hoped the answers would come to her, but the bell above the door cut her break short.

Taking a gulp of her tea, she wondered why silence had fallen on the café.

Pushing through the beaded curtain to investigate, she was as surprised as everyone else to see Hilda Heyward standing in the open doorway. Her two days in jail were clear from her dishevelled white hair, as well as the exhausted stare behind the glasses perched on her nose.

Unperturbed by the glares of her customers, Julia made her way through the crowd and reached Hilda's side. People scraped their chairs away, their suspicious gazes avoiding the woman who'd been a prime target of their gossip all morning. Hilda clutched the backs of chairs for support as she wobbled to the counter with Julia right by her side, and Julia locked eyes with anyone brave enough to glare. Julia was disappointed but not surprised, considering her gran's emphasis on the castor bean plants and break-in revenge motive.

What surprised her was how quickly her gran seemed to have forgotten that she'd been the one to ask Julia to help Hilda.

"It'll be someone else tomorrow," Julia assured her as she parted the beads. "Take a seat. Are you hungry? Thirsty?"

Hilda shook her head, climbing onto a stool as

though it pained her. Julia poured her a glass of water anyway before sitting next to her.

"You've been through a lot. I'm sorry that I had anything to do with that."

Hilda took a sip of water, her hands trembling. "It's been a nightmare, Julia. I never thought I'd be suspected of such a terrible thing. And I don't blame you. Not anymore. I was idiotic thinking I could hide such a large part of the story from the police. Reckless for thinking the break-in didn't matter."

A million and one questions rushed forward in Julia's mind, but she could feel the straining of the ears, the café still quiet despite the fervent whispering.

"You believe I didn't do it, don't you, Julia?" Hilda stared at her with those same hurt eyes from their first meeting, more desperate than ever. "I didn't know they were castor bean plants. I pay someone to tend my garden, you see. My Jack always sorted it before he passed. Running the food bank at my age, I never had the time or the energy. What Ronnie took from me wasn't worth killing over. Not to me, anyway."

"You know what he took?"

Glancing at the beads, Hilda nodded.

"*I* don't believe you killed Ronnie," Julia said. "And I know you didn't kill Georgiana. And once the truth is out there, so will everyone else."

An appreciative smile wobbled across her lips, transforming into quick tears. Julia ripped off a length of kitchen roll and handed it to Hilda to dab at her eyes. "I'm not so sure. I fear my reputation has been damaged by my recklessness. Oh, Julia, I've done something dreadful."

In the same whispered tone, Julia asked, "Does this have anything to do with you telling Paige to sell her flat?"

Hilda's eyes widened, mortified that Julia knew such a detail. She nodded, then took a deep breath before speaking. "It does. I never wanted to drag you into *this* mess. This isn't *me*, you see. Not really. Oh, I'm in so far over my head, I don't know what to do."

"You don't have to do anything right now. Rest, recover, and leave this to me."

"You're *still* willing to help me?" Hilda scrubbed away more tears. "Julia. I don't know what to say. I—"

"You don't have to say anything, either. Not now, at least. Are you free around six?"

Hilda wiped her tears and sniffed. "I should be. I have a meeting with a man claiming to be Ronnie's lawyer this afternoon. He was waiting for me outside the station when I was released. Wouldn't say what it was about. I should have pushed, but I couldn't believe they let me go. I thought someone had framed me so well that they'd believe it and I'd be spending my final years withering away behind bars, and the food bank—"

"Donations are still coming in," Julia assured her, pointing to the boxes from earlier waiting on the counter. "Come back tonight after the café closes, and we'll figure this out together. We can talk more in private. I promise you, Hilda, I'll do everything I can to help clear your name."

Hilda managed a weak smile. "Thank you, Julia. You're my guardian angel right now, and I don't deserve it. Can I leave through the back? I'm not sure I can endure another walk of shame."

Julia eased Hilda off the stool and walked her to the back door. Pausing on the step, Hilda stared out through the open gate at the field stretching out as far as the eye could see, and a soft smile lit up her face. "I haven't been around these parts in such a long while, but I'm *certain* that's where the old market hall used to be."

The detail surprised Julia, one she'd never heard in all her years at the café. "Really?"

"Would have been long before your time." Stepping off the doorstep, Hilda scanned the back of the café. "This would have been the toy shop?"

Julia shared Hilda's smile. "Was still the toy shop when I was growing up. And then a phone shop before I took it over."

"My parents had a fruit and veg stall at the market," she said. "I'd sit on the counter and the customers would hand me the money, and then I'd pass it to my mother. She was a whiz with numbers, and my dad had green fingers. There'd be times when people wouldn't hand me money, but my father would still give them what they needed. That always confused me, until one day I plucked up the courage to ask why, and my dear father said, 'Hilda, if people are brave enough to ask for help during troubled times, be brave enough to give it if you can.'" Her gaze drifted far beyond the field, but her smile only grew. "I met my Jack there too. He was a farmer, and I fell in love with him the moment he carried in that first crate of potatoes. Looked just like a young Richard Burton, you see. Oh, I miss him so much." Her eyes misted over, and she made for the gate. "I'll meet you here tonight, at six?"

"Tonight, at six," Julia confirmed, stepping back into the kitchen. "And Hilda, I need you to promise me something. When you come back, be as open as you were just then. No more secrets or filtering what you think is or isn't important. If you want my help to crack this case, I need to know everything."

With a promise that Julia had her word, Hilda shuffled off to her appointment with Ronnie's lawyer, leaving Julia to take the baked scones out of the oven.

She wasn't sure if she could deliver what she'd just promised Hilda, but she would not stop until she had the truth.

Whoever killed Ronnie and Georgiana, wherever they were, had to be thinking they'd got away with it. Certain the answer lay somewhere in her notes, Julia flipped back to the beginning, not going to let them get away with murder for a third time.

17

Jessie and Veronica drove the short drive to Fern Moore, where the sandwiches at Daphne's were as delicious as Billy had promised. She'd hoped to see him, not having heard from him since they'd parted during the chaos at Richie's. Benedict wasn't handing out his flyers either. Daphne, hoping they'd seen the back of Benedict for good, pointed them in the direction of Platts to find Norman.

"After what he's been saying about Ronnie, he's barred for life!"

Nestled behind the flat blocks, Platts Social Club stood alone across a deserted car park, the lingering Christmas lights around the peeling sign giving the dated club its own sort of Fern Moore charm. Inside, a handful of older men nursing afternoon pints cast curious glances at the newcomers. There wasn't much of an atmosphere to speak of, the sound effects of the slot machine filling in for the lack of music.

"Let's blend in," Veronica said, digging in her pocket for change. "What are you drinking?"

"Pass," Jessie said. "Norman's over there. You get your drink, I'll get him warmed up. And be warned, he's grumpy."

They split up, and Jessie approached Norman, deep in mumbled conversation with the machine. He hadn't been put together when she'd first met him, but he looked even shabbier with a few more days of white stubble growth. Too engrossed in his quest for a fortune, he didn't notice Jessie until she leaned against the machine.

"You again," he grumbled. "You got me barred from the café."

"That's not quite how I remember it, Norman. Won yet?"

"Leave me alone."

"We need to talk."

"About what?" He dug in his right pocket, and then his left, before checking the right again. "I don't have time for this."

Veronica returned with a bottle of cider, which surprised Jessie; she seemed more like a wine person.

She thumbed the change in her palm before passing it into Jessie's outstretched hand.

"Seems like you have nothing but time," Jessie said, holding out a shiny pound coin. "Have your last game on me."

Norman didn't think twice and snatched the coin from Jessie, rapid-firing it straight into the slot.

"Heard about the second poisoning?" Jessie asked, hoping it would be a long game.

"Didn't know her."

"Strange she'd die so soon after your brother."

"I told you, I know nothing about that. I'm glad he's gone. Good riddance."

Jessie leaned in closer and whispered, "Do you mean that?"

"You with the police or something?" Norman shot back.

"We're journalists," Veronica spoke up from the table she'd taken behind Norman. "We're just looking for the truth, Norman."

Something in his demeanour softened, and for a moment, Jessie thought he might let his guard down, but he went back to stabbing the buttons. "Didn't I already tell you I know nothing? Clear off."

"You were here on Friday, around lunchtime," Veronica pushed.

Suspicion flickered in Norman's eyes. "Who told you that?"

"Does it matter?" Jessie said. "But you don't deny it. Ronnie was here too, having lunch with someone. Chicken pie and mash, wasn't it?"

"It's always chicken pie and mash."

"Ronnie could have been poisoned here during that lunch," Veronica said, squinting at the column behind Jessie next to the machine. "Who was he with, Norman?"

"Some woman. I dunno."

"What woman?"

"I said I don't know."

"What did she look like?"

Norman beat both fists down on the machine. "Go away. I don't have to tell you anything. You've got nothing on me."

Jessie and Veronica exchanged glances.

"You were seen later that night, too," Jessie said. "Pounding on his door."

Norman froze, clinging onto the edge of the machine with both hands. "I don't know what you're talking about."

"You were caught on camera," she whispered. "Ronnie didn't answer, did he? Did you see anything, Norman?"

"He wasn't in."

"So, you admit to banging on his door?" Veronica said, dragging the bottle from her mouth. "He was already dead in there watching TV."

"The telly wasn't on, and I just told you, he wasn't in," Norman said, and Veronica pulled out her phone, excusing herself. Alone with Jessie, he continued, "That flat should have been *mine*. I'm the older brother. It should've been left to me, not Ronnie. He didn't need it, not with all that money they threw at him when he quit."

"Must have been a lot for you to be this upset about it."

"£40,000," Norman spat the numbers out, staring at the machine's flashing lights with no more coins to keep playing. "And he didn't share a single penny with me."

Shocked by the admission, Jessie looked around for Veronica, but she was nowhere to be seen.

"Did he keep that money in his safe?" Jessie asked.

"I know nothing about a safe."

For once, Jessie believed him. He looked far from a man who'd just come into money, and it would have been impressive if he'd gambled it all away on the Fern Moore slots already. Norman grumbled something about Ronnie owing him, but Jessie was tired of hearing it.

"Why should he have given you anything,

Norman? Look at yourself and what you're doing. Do you think this is healthy?"

In an instant, Norman had Jessie pinned up against the machine by her denim jacket. Pure rage replaced the weary glassiness in his eyes. A few years ago, she'd have already hit him so hard he'd have tumbled backwards over the table, but she did nothing. Norman let go as quickly as he'd grabbed hold and ran for the door. Catching her breath, Jessie tugged her jacket straight and wondered if she'd taken things too far again. She'd known Norman had a temper; he'd done the same thing to Ronnie in the same place, and Ronnie had reacted the same, like he'd known his brother wouldn't follow through.

"You all right, love?" the barmaid called.

"Yeah, I'm fine," Jessie said, kicking away from the machine. "Did you see where the woman with the giant glasses went?"

The barmaid nodded to the door, so Jessie wasted no time getting out of Platts. The afternoon light blinded her after being in the dim club. Veronica was pacing at the far end of the car park with the phone to her ear. A puff of smoke distracted Jessie on her way to catch up with her. Vaping against a lamppost, DI Moyes caught her eye as a car with blaring music cruised past.

"Talked to your mum this morning?" Moyes asked.

"No, why?"

"Then I'll tell you myself." She tucked her vape into her pocket and said, "Sorry about the other day. Talking over my day with Roxy made me realise how harsh I was with you. She said you were a good kid, and well, you're not even a kid, are you? You found Georgiana when we couldn't."

"I got lucky. Georgiana didn't."

"No, she didn't, did she?" Moyes sighed, glancing at Platts. "Bit early for a drink, isn't it? Or were you in there talking to Norman? He just shot out like a bat out of hell."

"So what if I was?"

"Feisty, aren't you?" Moyes looked amused. "Get anything from him? Can't seem to get more than a grumble."

Jessie considered telling her everything, but she bit her tongue, not sure if she accepted the apology yet. Besides, she had questions of her own.

"What was in the safe?"

Moyes rolled her eyes. "We don't know."

"Money?" Jessie asked. "You can tell that sort of stuff, can't you? Those new plastic notes we have must leave behind a trace, right?"

"Polymer, and yes, they do. And no, the safe wasn't filled with money. Like I said, we're still trying to figure that part out." Folding her arms, she asked, "Why do you—"

"*Detective!*"

Jessie turned to see PC Jake Puglisi sprinting across the car park.

"Can't you see I'm having a conversation, Puglisi?"

"Sorry," he said, panting for breath as he slowed to a halt, "but you told me to come and find you as soon as toxicology got in touch. They've been in touch."

"Spit it out, Jake."

"You were right about the macarons." Wiping his sweaty face, he glanced at Jessie. "The macarons were filled with poison. Ricin again, Detective."

It took all of Jessie's strength to stay upright. Moyes frowned at her, steadying her with a helping hand.

"I took her those macarons," Jessie said, her mouth drying out. "They were left on the doorstep, and I took them up to her."

"*What?*"

Tears stung Jessie's eyes. "I used them as my way to get into her apartment."

"You left that out of your statement," Puglisi said smugly. "Want me to cuff her?"

"Take your break, Police Constable," Moyes snapped, eyes clenched as though she couldn't organise her thoughts. PC Puglisi left them. "Julia is going to kill me for this. Jessie, you'll need to come to the station for questioning."

Unable to look up from the ground, Jessie followed DI Moyes towards the shadow of the flats.

"What's going on?" Veronica asked as they walked past her. "Has something happened?"

"It *was* my fault," Jessie called at her. "If I'd stayed out of this, she'd still be alive."

"Jessie, what's happened?"

Before Jessie climbed into the back of DI Moyes' sleek car, she dug into her pocket and tossed the ID badge onto the concrete. She hadn't wanted it in the first place. Not really.

"My contact confirmed Norman was right," Veronica called. "Ronnie might not have been in his flat when he was banging on the door. He didn't die in that chair. He was placed there."

Moyes slammed the car door, locking Jessie inside. "Unless the station releases information, I don't want to read about it in your paper. Do you understand? You've done enough damage to my investigation."

Jessie had just wanted to help solve what happened to Ronnie, but Moyes was right. She'd only made things worse.

18

*J*ulia was wiping one of the few empty tables when Veronica hurried into the café. Before the door had finished shutting, she burst out with, "They've arrested Jessie."

"*Arrested?*"

The word left Julia and bounced back at her like a stray bullet as a sudden hush descended over the café. She clutched the table to keep herself upright, the new target of her customers' silent staring. Her gran had left to walk the dogs, no longer there to divert their attention.

"The macarons she found on the doorstep at Wellington Heights were poisoned," Veronica said, a little quieter.

Julia was about to respond when a voice cut

through the room, dripping with venomous delight. "Hear that, everyone? Julia's daughter poisoned that woman at Wellington Heights!" Ethel White announced to the room.

A ripple of gasps echoed through the café. Half of the customers rose to their feet, their faces a mixture of shock and morbid fascination, while the other half stuck around waiting for the next development.

Veronica looked around, deflating as though she'd only just realised the impact of her entrance.

"Julia, I'm so sorry," she said quieter, pulling her to the counter. "I feel responsible. If I hadn't encouraged Jessie so much to join the newspaper, she would never have gone looking for Georgiana. I saw so much potential in her, just like you did when you hired her at the café. I just..."

Julia's heart pounded. Every word Veronica uttered was another bombshell. "*Join* the paper? I thought she was just helping you out. I didn't know."

All around her, the café continued to buzz with speculation at the drama unfolding before them.

"The café's closing," Julia announced, yanking off her apron and grabbing her bag. "Sorry, everyone. Family emergency."

There were some grumbled protests, but the gossipers who'd come for the show at Richie's funnelled out one by one. Julia followed Veronica out, locking the door behind them.

"Jessie mentioned you were confused about that chair being taken from Ronnie's flat," Veronica said as she caught up with Julia as she strode up the street towards the police station. "Ronnie didn't die in that chair. He was moved *after* he died. You'd think that would make it easier for the police to find the killer, right? But according to my station contact, they can't find any evidence of him being moved there."

Julia nodded, her mind otherwise occupied.

"Few working cameras in the area," Veronica continued, "and if someone saw something, they're not coming forward."

They reached the small police station across from The Plough, and to Julia's relief, DI Moyes was standing outside.

"I need to see Jessie."

Moyes sighed, and said, "I was just about to come and see you. I understand your concern, Julia, but Jessie isn't under arrest. She's here for voluntary questioning."

Julia was eased a little to know it was voluntary. "I won't leave until I know she's okay."

"I'm sorry, but that's not possible. Jessie isn't here right now."

"What do you mean, she's not here?" Julia's concern flared up again.

"She's at North Cotswolds Hospital having some tests," Moyes said, her expression solemn. "She admitted to chewing one of the ricin-laced macarons, but she spat it out before swallowing."

The thought of her daughter ingesting such a dangerous substance made Julia feel dizzy, and both Veronica and Moyes steadied her.

"It's just a precaution," Moyes said, clutching Julia's elbow. "Like I said, she spat it out."

Fighting back tears, Julia tried to focus her racing thoughts. "If someone left the poisoned macarons on Georgiana's doorstep, there should be cameras, right?"

"You'd think so, but no. A bakery in Riverswick made the macarons, and a third-party delivery company dropped them off at Wellington Heights. Judging by the time the delivery driver marked the order as complete and Jessie's arrival, they were waiting there for about two hours. Anyone could have tampered with them."

"Why are there no cameras?" Veronica interjected. "Are you telling me that James Jacobson cut corners with the security?"

"That's what I'm saying."

Julia wasn't there to stand around talking about cameras and James Jacobson. At that moment, she couldn't make herself care about anything more than Jessie.

"I need to go to her."

"I'm going to advise you against going there. The officers won't let you see her until she's given her official statement, and if you keep interfering, I might have to take further action."

"Oh, come on!" Veronica cried. "She's her mother. Are you being serious right now?"

Ignoring DI Moyes' warning and not looking for a pavement fight, Julia rushed back to her car parked in the alley next to the café. Her hands trembled as she tried to cram the key into the ignition. Veronica jumped into the passenger seat, and Julia turned to her, and tears streamed down her cheeks, "I can't lose Jessie."

"Moyes said it was just a precaution."

"But *poison*, Veronica?"

"Days ago," she reminded her. "She seemed fine when I saw her earlier."

Veronica's phone chimed. A sigh of relief escaped her as she checked it.

"She is fine, Julia," Veronica said with a laugh. "She still has her phone, so she's not under arrest. Tests have come back clear. Ended the text with 'Don't tell my mum.'"

Still clutching the wheel, Julia exhaled the panic

that had built up within. No wonder Jessie had wanted to keep it from her. She'd reacted as Jessie would have expected, and she let out a relieved laugh of her own.

"Who's behind all of this, Veronica?" Julia asked, able to twist the key with a calmer grip. "Norman, Paige, Audrey, Benedict... any of them could have killed Ronnie. But which one had a motive to want to kill Georgiana too?"

"I wish I knew. The more we dig, the more confusing it becomes."

They sat in silence for a moment with the rumbling engine, and Julia could feel how panicked Veronica had been. She didn't know her new neighbour all that well yet, but they shared a love for Jessie, and that was enough for Julia.

"We're going to the hospital anyway," Julia said. "Even if we can't see Jessie, we can still be there for her."

⁓

Later in the afternoon, after dropping Veronica off at Fern Moore to keep digging, Julia returned to her cottage, her mind swirling with the frustration of the day. She tossed her keys onto the side table and fought back a yawn. Barker appeared from the dining room, and she was glad not to be returning to an empty house.

"I thought you'd be at the café," Barker said.

"I closed early," Julia replied, sinking into the armchair she'd slept in. "Don't freak out, but Jessie's been taken to the station for questioning. And that was after she was taken to the hospital. They wouldn't let me see her at either place."

Barker's eyes widened. "What?"

Julia explained how the afternoon had gone, and chasing Barker back into the hallway, she had to do everything to stop him from leaving to go through the same motions she had at the station.

"They have *no* grounds to hold her," he cried, lingering by the front door. "This is ridiculous. They can't prove she knew anything about the poison. What's Moyes playing at?"

"I don't know."

"She's desperate, that's what," he said. "And I could throttle James Jacobson right now. Who builds luxury apartments and then doesn't pay for cameras? One brief clip of whoever poisoned those macarons could put an end to this."

"It's not like he's around to take the heat for that."

"Maybe not right now. Did you notice the scaffolding being taken down from the new house down the lane? They've been at it since lunchtime."

Julia shook her head, not remembering much of the drive home. "I don't think I was paying much attention to anything. How did your trip to Oxford go?"

"I wish I could say I found something, but Benedict Langley's alibi seems to hold up. I had to bribe a few staff members to get them to talk, but I got enough accounts of him over the three days he was there to rule out a two-hour round trip, plus any time he might have spent at Fern Moore. He was at the hotel from the moment he checked in until he left."

Julia sighed, feeling like the case was slipping through her fingers. "I don't know what I'm missing, Barker, but why does it feel like everything is just beyond my reach?"

"Just beyond your reach means you're closer than you think," he said, wrapping a comforting arm around her shoulder. "Did you hear about Hilda? They released her without charge."

Julia looked at the clock, having forgotten all about agreeing to meet Hilda in an hour. "She came into the café earlier. People acted like Jack the Ripper was walking Among them. Wouldn't be surprised if similar rumours are spreading about Jessie right now." Exhaling at her weary reflection in the hallway mirror, she said, "I should get back to the café. Hilda's going to tell me what Ronnie stole from her house.

Can you believe all of this started with a simple break-in?"

"Want me to come with you?"

Julia considered her response for a moment, but she shook her head. "I think she's expecting me on my own. Apparently, I'm her guardian angel."

"Not just Hilda's," he said through the mirror, hugging her from behind. "If anyone can figure this out, it's you, Julia."

19

At ten minutes past six, Julia's fingers began drumming on the middle table in the café as she watched the hands shudder around the clock. She wished she could reach out and slide them back, all the way to Saturday morning. That's when everything had last seemed normal, her biggest problems juggling orders, her gossiping gran, and some tea leaves in a cup.

From the moment Hilda turned up at the nursery window, everything had flipped upside down. Looking at the clock again, Julia couldn't believe Hilda wasn't at the café.

Hilda had given her word.

Did it mean anything?

The food bank owner had flip-flopped on Julia so

many times already, as inconsistent as Moyes' investigation. She couldn't believe Jessie was still at the station either, or that the officers at the desk were still claiming she was there voluntarily after so many hours.

If Barker was right about Moyes being desperate, Julia wouldn't stand for her daughter being used like a piece of old chewing gum pulled off a shoe to plug the holes in her investigation. Roxy's girlfriend or not, if Jessie wasn't released before midnight, Julia wasn't going to roll over and take it. She'd considered calling Roxy to ask her to put some pressure on Moyes, but she hadn't been able to bring herself to put her friend in that situation. Her backup plan, driving her car through the wall to break her out had always been cast aside.

Moyes wasn't the only one who was desperate.

All she could do was wait.

Too restless to sit down anymore, Julia began pacing back and forth across the café. She needed to make sense of the tangled web of motives and suspects cluttering her mind. Grabbing a stack of blank paper from behind the counter with a marker pen, she started organising her thoughts away from her notepad. She started jotting down names and clues, arranging them on the empty tables.

Audrey, the frustrated volunteer at the food bank,

stood out in her mind. She seemed to hold some grudge against Ronnie and didn't hide her dislike of Georgiana for her privileged life. Not the strongest motives for murder, but a place to start.

Then there was Paige, Ronnie's next-door neighbour, harbouring resentment against Ronnie for inspiring Josh to join the army. Paige had kept secrets and dodged the police, but what could have driven her to kill Georgiana?

Next on the table was Benedict, the property developer, and Georgiana's potential love interest. No one had a good word to say about him, but his alibi was rock-solid if Barker's afternoon in Oxford was anything to go by. He'd lied about not knowing Ronnie, only to admit that Ronnie assaulted him and that he'd wanted to discredit him.

And who was LB?

Julia's thoughts then turned to Hilda, and if she was going to write anything about her at all. The sweet and caring woman who sometimes displayed a snappy and aloof side. Twenty minutes past the hour, and she was still nowhere to be found. Julia had trusted Hilda from the beginning, despite Jessie's instincts.

Hilda got her own table too.

And finally, there was Norman, quick to anger and jealous of Ronnie's army money. Could Norman have figured out the combination to the safe, as Julia suspected? But again, what could be his motive for killing Georgiana?

As Julia looked at the spread-out papers, she felt overwhelmed, no clearer than the notes in her notepad. Each piece of the puzzle lead to a dead end, and she couldn't see a clear path through.

Just then, the café door opened, and Julia's chest leapt with hope. She expected to see Hilda, but her hope turned to joy when Jessie walked in, followed by Katie. Julia weaved around the tables and grabbed her daughter tight. Her friendship with Roxy would survive the night, as would her car and the station's walls.

"I'm so relieved," Julia said when she let go.

Jessie gave a reassuring smile. "I'm fine, Mum. Katie helped settle things."

"I drove her to the manor, and I saw the box already on the doorstep," Katie said, casting her eye over the notes. "Which meant the poison was already in the macarons when she picked it up and took them in, which I also saw her do as I was driving away. I knew I should have swallowed my pride and come in with you, Jessie."

"And I shouldn't have stuck my nose in. It's my fault I got dragged into it."

Julia brushed a strand of hair away from Jessie's

face. "You were only trying to help. This isn't your fault."

Jessie's eyes landed on the investigation notes, and she started reading over them, her brow furrowing in thought. Katie leaned in to read the Benedict table, her plump lips tracing along with the words.

"That's not right," Katie said, tapping a sheet with a long nail. "Langley is the name of the woman Georgiana's dad married. The one who bled him dry. They weren't a couple."

"Georgiana and Benedict were step-siblings?" Julia confirmed.

"Don't you remember, Jessie?" Katie said. "When you came to have your nails done. I told you all about it."

"You didn't mention their names."

"Didn't I?" Katie's lips curled outwards. "Well, I never knew Benedict's name. I just heard that Georgiana had an awful new family that ruined her father's life with how they wasted his money."

"Explains the bickering at the café," Julia said, adding the correction. "Could they have been involved in Benedict's plans together?"

Katie shook her blonde curls. "I doubt it. I think Georgiana kept her distance. Listen, I need to get back to Vinnie, but your father and I can keep Olivia for the night to give you space to figure this out."

Julia smiled, giving Katie a hug. "Thank you, that would be a great help."

"Any time," Katie said. "And pop into the salon as soon as you're free. I say this with love, but you're in desperate need of an emergency exfoliating facial."

Katie left, and after checking her pallid complexion in the back of a spoon, the two of them stood over the tables, reading over all the notes again. Jessie had added some more notes. Benedict ruined a property portfolio in Cornwall before moving to the Cotswolds, and Norman claimed Ronnie had £40,000, which DI Moyes was certain wasn't what was taken from his safe.

Julia took a deep breath and broached the subject she'd been hesitant to discuss. "So, the newspaper?"

"Veronica told you then."

"Shouldn't she have?"

Jessie shrugged, half turning away from her. "Stupid idea. Not even mine. Johnny suggested it before he left, and I was just going along with it, and look where it got me."

For all her denial, Jessie's conflict was clear.

"If you want to chase this," Julia said softly, "you know I'll be the *first* person cheering you on. Every time. No matter what."

"We've only just got used to Sue working at the café."

"We'd figure things out, just like we did before."

"Yeah, well, I've messed it up now, so it's not happening."

"Don't think Veronica wouldn't want you anymore because of what happened. She was just as worried about you. She cares a great deal about you, Jessie."

"I threw my ID back at her."

Julia walked around the counter and retrieved her handbag. She pulled the ID out and carefully placed it on the counter. Jessie glanced at it, but only out of the corner of her eye.

"Veronica feels just as responsible," Julia said. "We had a lot of hours to sit around talking today trying to get answers about why you were being held. We both agreed that the sky is the limit for you, Jessie, you just have to get out of your own way. You've already done so many things you never thought you would. Look at what you've just done at a college. That wasn't easy for you, and you didn't give up."

"Probably failed them all, anyway."

"Now, I doubt that," Julia said, raising both eyebrows. "Where's that girl who came back from seeing the world, full of pearls of wisdom, ready to take on any challenge? Don't let what happened to Georgiana define your path."

Jessie's expression softened, and she looked down

at the ID. "You know I don't want to leave the café, right?"

"And if you did, I wouldn't mind," she assured her. "I'd miss you here, but you have nothing to prove to me. You know I'll always be here for you, no matter what you decide." But something on Benedict's table had distracted Jessie halfway through what Julia was saying. "What is it?"

"Who's 'LB'?"

"Your dad found Benedict's diary," Julia said. "He's noticed his chair is missing, by the way."

"Did you tell him I had it?"

"What do you take me for?"

"You've been spending too much time around Fern Moore," Jessie said, her playful smile lifting Julia's spirits. "And good, because if you do, I'll tell him you helped me carry it up to my flat. It's comfy. LB?"

"Someone Benedict had three meetings with over the week leading up to Ronnie's death," she said. "It might not even be connected to the case."

The café door opened again, and Hilda arrived, forty minutes late. She was apologetic, explaining that her meeting with Ronnie's lawyer had taken longer than expected. Julia sat her down, making her a pot of tea and serving it with some banana bread. Hilda looked dismayed to see her name on a table.

"I thought you believed me?" she asked, taking a bite of the banana bread to compose herself. "I suppose I did it to myself."

"It's been a tough day," Julia said, sitting across from her while Jessie flipped a chair around and straddled it backwards. "I wanted to cover all bases. So, Hilda, let's cut to the chase. You promised you'd be honest with me. What did Ronnie steal from your house?"

Hilda's hands trembled as she picked up another piece of banana bread, trying to steady herself. Her eyes darted between Julia and Jessie.

"I didn't figure out what Ronnie took until the day *after* we found him," Hilda confessed, her voice wavering with nervousness. "He took some paperwork from a dining room drawer."

All this secrecy for paperwork?

That would have been the day Hilda had been so aloof with her.

She'd chalked it up to grief and exhaustion.

"What kind of paperwork?"

"Is this about you pressuring Paige to sell her flat?" Jessie pushed when Hilda didn't respond.

"I wouldn't say *pressuring*. I just wanted to help."

"You were working with Benedict, weren't you?" Jessie said, shaking her head. "I don't believe it. I knew there was something off about you."

"Please, you must believe me. He seemed so different when he first turned up," she pleaded. "He claimed he wanted to transform the place for the better, you see, to help people. That's all I've ever wanted to do there."

Jessie interjected, "But his actual plan is to turn the flats into holiday rentals, isn't it? Like he did in Cornwall?"

Hilda nodded. "I'm afraid so. And I swear, I didn't know his true intentions at first, or else I would never have agreed to help him. I regret *ever* agreeing to work with him. But by the time I realised what kind of man he was, it was too late, and how could I stop him? I used to work for the council in the planning department. He wasn't doing anything illegal."

"Immoral, though," Jessie muttered. "So, he hired you as his bulldog to force people out?"

"It wasn't like *that*," Hilda insisted, clenching her eyes. "I didn't know he was going to offer people so little. You must understand, I thought it was for the best. I thought it would mean fewer mouths to feed, and it would help people move on to better places. So many people inherited those flats, it would have been pure profit for them. Only two of the families who sold to him were my doing, and when I found out how much he rushed through the process, I told him I didn't condone his practices and I backed out of our arrangement."

"Was he paying you?" Julia asked.

Hilda sipped her tea before offering a meek nod.

"It was a small commission," she explained. "And I put *every* penny into the food bank. I hate to say it, but it helped us survive a partially difficult fortnight."

"If he wants to turn Fern Moore into a holiday destination, it would turn the place into a ghost town," Jessie said. "Tourism is so seasonal around here, and no offence to the estate, but Peridale is at least pretty, and even we see the fluctuation every year. But you didn't care about any of that, did you?"

Hilda's eyes clenched, confirming Jessie's words. "I told you, I didn't know those details at first. He made it sound so charitable. You don't understand how thinly we've been stretched. The second he showed me the digital renderings of his vision for the place, I told him he needed to stop. I couldn't undo my part in convincing those two families to trust him."

Hilda took a deep breath, neither Jessie nor Julia seeming to know what to say.

"After my confrontation with Benedict," Hilda continued, "I thought maybe he was backing out of the plan when I saw the flats were staying empty. I just wanted it all to stop, but Ronnie overheard our conversation. He already hated all the developers sniffing around the place after Wellington Heights reeled them all in, signalling that there were profits to be made in the area. Ronnie confronted me about why I'd help Benedict, and I made another mistake. I denied everything. We were so close, I didn't want to disappoint him."

"Master of spin, right?" Jessie said, almost under her breath.

"I wanted to soften things," Hilda said, not hearing Jessie, "and I thought suggesting him for the front page of the newspaper would show him I wasn't like Benedict, that I only cared about the food bank. Ronnie *was* the saviour of the food bank, but he was smart. He saw right through me. I felt such a kinship with him, and he became so disappointed in me. And the more flats people sold to Benedict, the more upset he was with me. I should never have had a single conversation with Benedict, but I was just becoming so jaded with the struggles of the food bank and the constant trouble at Fern Moore."

Julia nodded, understanding the complexity of the situation despite Jessie's glaring. "I can imagine how difficult it must have been for you."

Hilda struggled a weak smile. "When Ronnie attacked Benedict, I tried to warn Ronnie to leave it alone, but he insisted he needed to find proof of

Benedict's plans. He was going to get another front page of the paper to expose Benedict's desire to clear out the estate for his own benefit. But with the flats empty and people still selling, there wasn't much he could do."

"And that's when he broke into your house," Julia said.

Hilda nodded. "If I'd been honest with him, maybe he wouldn't have gone looking."

"As messed up as all of this is," Jessie said, "how did this lead to Ronnie's death?"

"That's the part I still don't understand," Hilda admitted. "Benedict was out of the village during the poisoning."

Looking over the tables, a thought occurred to Julia.

"What if he had an accomplice?"

"Like Georgiana?" Jessie suggested. "They were step-siblings, and maybe she helped poison Ronnie with a cupcake, then threatened to expose Benedict and he killed her?"

"Georgiana? Step-siblings?"

"Her rich father married his mother," Julia confirmed. "But I'm not convinced Georgiana would help Benedict kill Ronnie. She wanted to be on the newspaper's cover instead of him, but that's no reason to kill. And her father was still paying for her lifestyle, so she didn't need any money Benedict could give her."

Jessie's mouth formed a perplexed frown, climbing out of the chair to walk Among the notes. "Then what are we missing? There has to be something else. Does LB mean anything to you, Hilda?"

"I don't think so."

"And did Paige have any conflict with Georgiana?"

"Paige had run-ins with everyone, but we cut her slack because of Josh. I don't see any reason for her to kill Georgiana, though. Maybe she found out something, but I can't see her as a killer."

Julia added, "I agree. Paige might have her issues, but poisoning seems too far for her. Norman might be a possibility, but he'd be more likely to resort to something violent given how he's been acting."

"Norman is a tricky case," Hilda said with a sad sigh. "You didn't hear this from me because I know he does not like to talk about it. *Ever*. But, many years ago, his daughter died far too young. She was born very sick, and his marriage didn't survive the fallout." She closed her eyes, as though the admission had drained her. "Ronnie wasn't the only broken Roberts brother, but there was never any getting through to Norman. I know Ronnie tried, but in the end, he had to give up on him. They both had the same temper as their father. Ronnie learned to keep it in check. He learned to control his vices. Norman gave up, and he keeps giving up every single day he's at one of those damned machines. Norman's wife was the love of his life, and so was his daughter."

Julia's heart sank, and they discounted Norman as a suspect. However, Jessie was still stuck on the initials. She paced the floor, repeating the letters over and over until they didn't sound like letters to Julia.

"Love," Jessie repeated. "What if it means 'love birds?'"

"Love birds?" Hilda echoed.

"It's something Benedict kept saying to me when I pretended I had a flat to sell because my imaginary boyfriend was scared of ghosts. 'You love birds deserve somewhere nice to live.'"

"Could be?" Julia said. "He might have had a lover. Hilda, did you know if he had any other relationships?"

"I didn't know him well. I wanted nothing to do with him after we went our separate ways."

"What about Ronnie?" Julia asked, not sure where she was going. "Did he have anyone special in his life?"

Hilda hesitated, fidgeting with her hands.

"Is there something you're not telling me, Hilda? Remember, secrets aren't helping this situation."

"It's nothing." Hilda sighed, busying herself with correcting the angle of the teacup. "Okay, fine. I saw Ronnie making a pass at Audrey during the Christmas party at Platts. I remember thinking it was just a silly drunken thing."

"But you said Ronnie didn't drink?"

"He was as sober as a judge, which made the whole thing seem so strange because Audrey has never shown that she likes him all that much, and—"

Hilda stopped, her eyes narrowing on the surface of her tea like one of Evelyn's predictions was bubbling to the surface. "No, it's nothing."

"Really, lady?" Jessie cried. "Whatever it is, spit it out. This isn't a game."

"The castor bean plants in my garden," Hilda started, fiddling with her wedding ring. "I never knew what they were until the police told me about them. My Jack planted them. He was always so much better. I paid a neighbour to tend to my garden."

"What neighbour?"

"That's not what I'm getting at," Hilda said, standing up and walking to the table with her notes. She picked up the note Julia had made about the ricin plants. "It's just ... now that I'm thinking about it, if the castor beans were picked from my garden, only one of these people has ever been to my cottage."

Julia raised an eyebrow, her mind working

through the possibilities, but only one name jumped out. Hilda had told her Audrey had slept on her sofa the night after Ronnie was found. She thought back to her last meeting with Audrey outside the food bank in the rain, recalling something she had said. "Hilda, do you think you could identify Audrey from an old photograph?"

"How old of a picture are we talking about?"

"From when she was a teenager?"

"I'm afraid I didn't know her then," she said, "but perhaps? I'd have to see it, obviously."

"I don't have it," Julia said, staring out of the café window in the far-off direction of the estate. "I don't suppose the police have put that key back under Ronnie's matt."

"We can bust down the door and worry about it later," Jessie said. "It's not like anybody lives there."

Hilda's hand fumbled around in her pocket and pulled out a keyring with a few tarnished keys.

"There's no need for either of those things. These keys are why I was so late today," she said, her voice cracking as tears welled behind her glasses. "I told you Ronnie was a good man and a wise one, too. He left his flat to the food bank under the agreement that it would be sold, and every penny of the profits would be donated to the food bank. Even from beyond the grave, you see, he's looking out for his own."

"Damn, Ronnie," Jessie exclaimed with a disbelieving laugh.

"Damn, indeed," Julia agreed, a lump in her throat. Tears clouded her vision as she snatched up her car keys from the table. "We need to get to Fern Moore right away."

As they rushed out of the café, Ronnie's selflessness drove Julia forward with a renewed determination to uncover the truth behind the poisoning.

She'd honour Ronnie's noble legacy by bringing his killers to justice, and she might have just figured things out.

But first, they needed to prove it.

∾

Julia drove to the flat at lightning speed under a hazy orange sky, giving Jessie just enough time to ask about the £40,000 Norman claimed Ronnie had tucked away somewhere.

"Ronnie never talked about money to me," Hilda stated, clinging onto the dashboard as Julia sped around a tight bend in the lane. "He seemed too proud and always had enough to get by. His lawyer mentioned the flat was his only asset, so if he had *that* much money, it wasn't in his will."

Or his bank account, Jessie would guess.

At Fern Moore, they ran up to Ronnie's flat and let themselves in, using Hilda's key. Julia flicked on the exposed bulb in the ceiling and hurried to the mantelpiece, but Jessie knew it wouldn't need three of them to stare at an old photograph. She hadn't even met Audrey, anyway. Still feeling the need to contribute, to set things right, Jessie began her search for clues in the bedroom.

Lacking any furniture aside from the basics and no hint of decoration, it wasn't the bedroom of a man with a fortune. Or at least, not the room of a man spending money on himself. She started in the wardrobe where the safe had been, but it had been cleared out, and if there were any hidden panels, her tracing fingertips didn't pick up on them.

Leaving the wardrobe, her eyes fell on an old, worn-out chest in the room's corner. She tried to lift the lid, but the hinges were well worn. With a determined grunt, she pried it open, snapping the lid off in the process to reveal damp-smelling army clothes. She dug around in the camouflage and stiff jackets, finding a tin full of medals hidden at the bottom, but no money.

Frustrated but undeterred, she turned her attention to a desk under the window. She rifled through old issues of *The Peridale Post*, his cover on the top, and opened drawers full of bits and bobs.

Nothing.

She didn't even know what £40,000 would look like.

What was she missing?

She settled on the threadbare rug in the middle of the floor. With a spark of hope, she ripped it back. Nothing, and the police would have checked there first.

Maybe she wasn't the first who'd come looking for the money, but how many people had known about it aside from Norman? She needed to think outside of the box.

On the streets, if you wanted to keep something safe, you kept it close. On you, if you could, but Ronnie wouldn't have been carrying that much money around with him. Not all at once, at least. If you were lucky to have a patch at the Fenton Industrial Estate with a sleeping bag, it meant you had places to hide things. Jessie used to keep her spare change in the lining. It would only rattle if people went looking for it, and there was always someone around to hear it to put a stop to the thieving.

Ronnie had stolen from them because he hadn't

wanted to beg. She'd thought he'd been too proud back then. Now she knew he'd been too broken.

Dropping to her knees, Jessie felt around under the single bed, her fingers grazing over dust and debris. She was about to give up her search, but something sticky on the underside of the mattress caught the back of her hand. She flipped the thin mattress over with a grunt to reveal a slash held together by a lattice of grey tape.

It came off like one of Katie's wax strips.

"Great hiding place, Ronnie," Jessie said as she reached inside the concealed compartment, her fingers trembling as they closed around something made of paper buried deep in the stuffing. She pulled out an envelope, and her eyes widened as she looked inside at even more envelopes, the money divided up.

"Georgiana was right about Ronnie not getting that many donations for the food bank," she said, running into the sitting room, "but I think the only person Ronnie was stealing from these days was his future self. There's still a lot here, but I bet if we counted it out, there'd be a chunk missing to cover everything he donated."

"Oh, Ronnie." Hilda's tears started fresh. "I never doubted you."

"No wonder he didn't give any to Norman," Jessie said, weighing it up. "He had other uses for it."

Julia strode across the room holding the photograph, the broken pieces of a frame on the floor behind her. Putting her phone to her ear, Julia handed the picture to Jessie. She'd never have recognised Ronnie from the man she'd known, but as Billy had pointed out, she'd never really known him.

With his arm around a girl with long brown hair on a bench with the flats in the background, he looked happier than she'd ever seen him. In the bottom right-hand corner, the old school camera had burned the date in blurry orange letters.

"February 5th 1986," Jessie read aloud. "Is the girl Audrey?"

"I think it could be," Hilda said, still uncertain. "She lived on the estate back then."

Julia pulled her phone down and took the picture. "DI Moyes isn't answering. After everything that's happened, I'm not surprised."

"Try Roxy," Jessie suggested.

Face lighting up, Julia typed out a message, and one fired back in an instant.

"They're at Richie's," she said. "We need to get back to the village."

"And Jessie, hold on to that money tight," Hilda said. "On second thoughts, put it back where you found it. Ronnie hid it well enough that the police missed it. The food bank inherited the contents of the flat too. He's just saved us for years to come."

Julia and Hilda rushed out of Ronnie's flat and Jessie returned to the bed to stuff the money back into the mattress. After putting everything back where she'd found it, she took one last look at the medals.

"Sorry I judged you, pal," she said, snapping the box shut and laying them on his uniforms. "At ease, soldier."

Jessie shut the flat door, her mum and Hilda already running across the courtyard. The door at the next flat opened, and bright red hair appeared.

"Oi, are you Billy's ex?" Paige asked, looking her up and down. "I just heard someone say 'Jessie' and he doesn't shut up about you."

Jessie nodded, surprised by the question. "What's going on?"

"You heard from Billy?"

"Should I have?"

"He was on his way to see you," she said, chewing at her lip as she glanced over the walkway. "Said he'd be back before the oven chips were cooked, but that was two hours ago."

"Did he say why?"

She shook her head. "I was in the bath. He shouted that he'd found something important and the next thing he was gone."

"Have you called him?"

"Had to sell my phone this morning to cover his share of the rent."

Jessie pulled out her phone, only to discover it was still on silent from her time at the station. There were eight missed calls from Billy, all from two hours ago, but nothing since. Panicked, she called him back, and he picked up after the first few rings.

"Billy? It's Jessie. Where are you?"

"I'm afraid it's not Billy," an unfamiliar voice said. "Hello, Jessie, I'm Doctor Williams, and I'm sorry to have to tell you like this, but Billy has been involved in a serious accident."

20

Julia hurried into Richie's and found DI Moyes and Roxy sitting in a corner booth. Behind the bar, Richie struggled a smile in their direction, off in his own world. Unsurprisingly, the bar was quiet given the previous night's events. Roxy looked concerned as Julia approached, while Moyes remained focused on her drink.

"I'm allowed a night off," Moyes said, twisting her glass around. "Just *one* night with my girlfriend."

"Watch how you talk to Julia," Roxy warned, tapping Moyes' arm. "It's clear she's here with something important. How's Jessie doing?"

"She's..." Julia glanced around, realising that she'd left Jessie behind when she drove off earlier, too preoccupied by her date. "She's fine. She's at Fern Moore, where we just came from. Moyes, we need your help."

Moyes sighed, and asked, "What do you need?"

Julia took a deep breath, pulling the picture out of her pocket.

"Barker found Benedict's diary," she began. "There didn't seem to be anything crucial to the case, except for references to meetings with someone only referred to as 'LB.' We didn't think much of it until tonight when Jessie made a connection. Does LB mean anything to you?"

"Should it?" Moyes asked, taking a sharp sip from her drink. "I'm tired of the games, Julia. I have the Chief Superintendent pushing to close this case, and it didn't even happen on *my* patch. I chose Riverswick for precisely this reason."

"Laura didn't get much sleep last night," Roxy whispered, rubbing Moyes' back. "Always makes her cranky. Who's LB, Julia?"

"We believe it stands for 'love birds,' based on something Benedict said to Jessie," Hilda replied. "We suspect he's behind all of this."

"He has an alibi. What's that in your hand?"

"A picture from Ronnie's flat."

"Are you telling me you broke into a dead man's flat?"

"We used the key," Hilda said. "It's now the food bank's flat."

Moyes squinted at her, downing her drink. She snatched the photograph from Julia and studied it. "So, what am I looking at?"

"The combination on the safe was 050286, right?"

Wide-eyed, Moyes tossed the picture down and leaned back with folded arms. "Either you're as psychic as the woman from the B&B, or I need to find out who's leaking information at the station."

"Look at the date in the corner."

Moyes glanced at it. "What's the relevance?"

"The girl in the picture. Did you find her?"

"Should we have?" Moyes glared, looking around the bar as though none of this was even happening. "Just some old teenage romance he never stopped clinging onto."

"A teenage romance important enough to Ronnie that he still had the picture on his mantelpiece after all these years," Julia said, jabbing the picture. "And if I was right about the combination, it was significant enough that he used that date for his safe. I thought Norman might have been the one to be able to guess any significant numbers, but there are other people in his life that he's known nearly as long. For him to keep this picture, I believe this might have been the last time he saw her before he left for the army."

"Left *who*?" Moyes demanded. "Who is the woman in the picture?"

"Benedict's accomplice," Julia said.

"It was Audrey all along," Hilda muttered, her brows deep in a frown. "She was the only one who'd been to my cottage before Ronnie broke in. The only one who would know I had those plants."

"Benedict has an alibi because he wasn't working alone," Julia continued, taking a deep breath. She held up the picture for DI Moyes, who seemed lost for words. "Audrey is the one who poisoned her 'love bird.'"

Roxy grinned. "See, I told you she's brilliant."

~

In the corridor outside of Billy's room in the hospital, Jessie couldn't look away from the window. Head poked out of a green sheet, with tubes sticking out everywhere, he looked so frail and small. Sue appeared at her side back from talking to the doctors, wrapping a hand around Jessie's.

"They're saying he's stable after the surgery," Sue said with a reassuring squeeze. "Skidded off his electric scooter on the lane to Peridale. He'll wake up sore with cracked ribs and a broken arm, but he'll be fine."

Jessie's eyes welled up with tears of relief, but she couldn't help but feel guilty. "It's my fault. He was only rushing on the scooter to show me something. If my phone hadn't been on silent—"

"Less of that, please," Sue said, her tone firm. "You couldn't have known this would happen. Accidents happened. I've seen a lot worse in these halls from electric scooter accidents. He's lucky an oncoming vehicle didn't hit him."

"I told him it wasn't safe."

"Then you were looking out for him," she said, nudging their arms together. "He isn't just going to wake up because you're standing here staring at him. Not yet, at least."

"I need to know what he found."

"And when he comes around, you can ask him yourself," Sue assured her. "Right now, he needs to rest, and so do you. I'll cover your shift at the café tomorrow but go home. Sleep. It's going to be a long night for Billy regardless."

"I can't leave him," Jessie insisted, her determination unwavering. "I'll stay here until he wakes up."

Sue looked like she was going to put up a fight, but she sighed and sat in the chair on the other side of the corridor. Patting the seat next to her, she said, "Then I'll be right here right with you."

"Aren't you tired of this place?"

"What's one more night?" Sue shrugged. "You know, I thought I missed it, but it turns out, I've never been happier than working at the café with you and your mum. No going back." Sue paused, and said, "Have you told her?"

"Mum will only worry," Jessie said, pulling herself away from the window to take the seat. "She's cracked the case."

"Never doubted she would. Now then, there's a vending machine around the next corner. Get us some coffee, and I'll keep watch."

Jessie found the vending machine and punched in the buttons, trying to make sense of the night and what Billy had found. If it had been important enough for him to jump on his scooter, it had to be connected to the case. But it didn't matter now. If her mum and Hilda had found Moyes, they'd be making arrests.

While the second coffee spluttered out, she thought about what Sue had just said about 'no going back.' She'd written something like that in her college personal statement too, written at the wedding after realising Billy had changed his number. He'd felt so far away, buried in her past, but he was here in a hospital bed clinging on to life. Very much her present, but she couldn't make sense of how she felt.

Everything since the bar had been a blur.

An intense blur.

And her heart ached.

"Doctor Williams, that file you asked for."

Looking away from the machine and blinking out of her confusion, Jessie turned to see a tall doctor hurrying down the corridor, slowing to accept a folder from a nurse. Picking up the coffee, Jessie ran after him and introduced herself.

"Ah, the girl on the phone," the doctor said with a solemn nod. "I'm sorry I had to let you know like that. Never a straightforward thing to say, always a harder thing to hear. He's doing a lot better than when he was brought in."

"Did he say anything?" Jessie asked, hurrying to keep pace. "Before he went into surgery?"

He shook his head. "Sorry, he was unconscious."

"Do you still have his phone?"

Doctor Williams patted down his pockets and pulled out a phone, its screen shattered. "Thing went flying by the looks of it. What relation to Billy are you?"

"Friend," she said.

The doctor hesitated, but after a glance at his watch, he thrust the device into Jessie's hand and hurried off. Returning to Sue with the coffee, she sat down, twirling the phone between her hands for a moment, unsure of what to do with it. The smell of the roasted beans reminded her too much of the martinis, and she put it under her chair.

"Does face ID still work when you have tubes sticking out of your mouth?"

"I don't know," Sue replied. "Going to check his messages?"

"Don't be gross."

Kicking off the chair, Jessie snuck into the hospital room, so much quieter than the corridor even with all the beeping. She forced herself not to break down again at seeing him in his state and held the phone up to his face. The device hesitated before unlocking.

Unsure of where to start, she apologised to Billy as she swiped up to see his used apps.

～

At the cottage, around the crackling fire at the bottom of the garden, Julia and Hilda roasted marshmallows on sticks, while Barker tapped on his laptop between them.

"My entire world has changed since I was last here," Hilda said, peeling off a layer of gooey sugar. "Feels like a lifetime ago."

"It does," Julia agreed, fixed on the dancing flames. "How's the organising going, Barker?"

"I think I have the timeline worked out," Barker said through a yawn, stretching out wide. "The police would be idiots to ignore all this fresh evidence."

The unexpected trio sat around the fire in silence for a while, with only Barker's tapping and the crackle of the fire as their backdrop. Julia had expected her mind to race, but after the night they'd had, she'd cleared the deck.

She was ready for things to end.

"Remember how I said Ronnie was there for me when no one else was?" Hilda said after a time, and Julia nodded. "Sitting around this fire, staring into the flames, I've just remembered the first night I felt like that. He'd been donating at the food bank for a while, but one night, on my way to the bus stop, I came across a fire at Fern Moore. It was in a bin, and people crowded around it like we are now." She pulled her hand up, thumbing her wedding ring. "That wasn't a good day for me, you see. I'd picked up Jack's ashes, and I couldn't see a way forward. I thought my life had ended when his life ended. Fifty years..."

She sniffed, and Barker closed his laptop, listening as closely as Julia.

"I stood around that fire, staring into the flames with strangers, and I sobbed. I cried so much, for so long, all the people who'd been there when I arrived left. And I couldn't stop myself. I don't think I wanted to, truth be told. I thought I was alone in the end, but I wasn't. Ronnie was there, on the other side of the flames. Silent, but he was there. I pulled off my ring." She repeated the action, rolling it in her palm. "I tossed it right into the fire. I don't know what I thought I was doing, but without a second thought, Ronnie kicked the bin over and stamped out the flames. He found my ring, cooled it off in a puddle, and put it back on my finger, and told me that no matter how much I tried, I'd never run away from who I was, no matter how much I wanted to. I gained a genuine friend that night, and now, he's just another person to miss. I let him down."

"I'm sure he wouldn't say that if he was here now," Julia said, staring into the flames. "A different fire, a different day, and you've gained some new friends. We're here for you, Hilda."

"Yeah, of course," Barker said. "Just please don't throw your ring into the fire again. I'm not sure I'm the dive-into-the-fire type."

Hilda chuckled and slipped the ring back on.

"It was a moment of madness that I don't care to repeat," she said. "It was that night I knew Ronnie had seen true darkness. You know, he never talked to me about any of it. What he saw. What he experienced. I don't think he talked about it to anyone. Not the specifics. He was so gentle with me, I just knew. I wanted so much to release him from that burden. I suppose he doesn't have it anymore, does he?"

"He doesn't," Julia said, reaching across to rub her thumb against Hilda's knee. "And soon, when all of this is put to bed, he'll be at peace."

Julia's phone pinged, disrupting the moment. She pulled it out, surprised to see a video message from Jessie with a cryptic 'Thank Billy' caption. Tilting her phone, she pressed play. The footage was dark and blurry, but recognised where it had been filmed from. As dark as it was, there was no mistaking the rattling sound of the shopping trolley.

"What's with the smile?" Barker asked.

"You have something else to add to your timeline," Julia said, "The last piece of the puzzle."

Julia played the video again for them both, and they both understood what it meant without her needing to explain.

"Then that settles it," Hilda said with a sigh. "What are we going to do?"

"Tonight? Nothing," Julia replied. "Is Audrey due in at the food bank tomorrow?"

"Tomorrow at noon."

"Hilda, you can have the sofa tonight," Julia said, pushing herself up from the log with a yawn. "This ends tomorrow at noon."

21

The following afternoon, in the food bank on the Fern Moore estate, the sun bled in through the open shutter, drenching the shelves in warm light. Dot and Percy had kept true to their word to continue gathering donations, keeping Julia and Hilda busy restocking for most of the morning.

"For their deeper pockets, the villagers around Riverswick are as tight as a mouse's ear," Dot announced to Julia after carrying in the last box. "I know it seems like more than yesterday, but they have *twice* as many houses as us, most of which are *twice* the size. Peridale comes out on top again, but no surprise there. I heard they cheated in our last bowls match, too."

"Every little helps," Julia reminded her.

"Hmm. You're rather quiet today."

"Am I?"

"Your gran can tell when something's going on, dear," she said, circling a finger around Julia's face. "You're supposed to be at the café today."

"Sue's got it covered for now. I'll be along later."

"How's Billy doing?" Dot persisted with the questions, despite Percy struggling to keep their dogs still on the other side of the shutters. "I heard he flew ten feet in the air and landed right on his head."

"Where'd you hear that?"

"I'll be surprised if the boy will ever string another sentence together," Dot said, pushing up her curls. "Not that he's the sharpest pencil in the box, mind you. Are they..." She jerked her head as though to insinuate something. "You know ... back together?"

"I don't think so."

"Good."

"Billy's not so bad, Gran."

"I never said he was," Dot carried on, fluttering her lids. "I didn't want to say anything because you know I'm not one to gossip, but I've been seeing him around the estate ever since I started volunteering. Not that he ever saw me. If he had, he might not have been so quick to stick his tongue down the throat of that unfortunate girl every chance he got. She had the ghastliest red hair I've ever seen." She glanced at

Percy, moments from having both arms dislocated. "Anyway, wish us luck not to get mowed down by a hooligan on a scooter on our walk back to the village."

Never failing to be surprised by her gran, Julia wished her luck and continued adjusting the cereal boxes, pulling the cornflakes to the front.

"I don't think she's coming," Hilda said to Julia in a brief lull at half past noon. "It's as if she's figured something out."

"Maybe the police got to her first?"

"Or she's taken a leaf from Georgiana's book and she's halfway to Timbuktu."

They continued to work until close to one when Audrey brushed into the food bank. Throwing her coat and bag on a nearby chair, she said, "It's been a day, let me tell you. Some ungrateful woman wouldn't accept the terms of the joint custody agreement, ignoring the fact she was lucky to be having *any* access to her children at all. And if I'd had my way, she wouldn't have. Some people would rather see their kids suffer than lose an inch of ground."

Exhaling as though the worst of the day was over, she looked around the food bank, landing on Julia with an accusing frown.

"I moved everything back to how it was for a *reason*. Your layout made everything more complicated."

"It works fine in my café," Julia said, remaining calm.

"Yes, well, we're not in *your* café, are we?"

Audrey turned her attention to the clipboard, too lost in her own frustration to notice Hilda couldn't look in her direction. Julia took out her phone and tapped out three text messages, and sent them one by one. She gave Hilda a covert thumbs up.

Now, they just had to wait as the food bank fell quiet once more, the only sound being Audrey's occasional huff of exasperation as she rearranged the shelves back to her liking.

～

Upon receiving the text from her mum, Jessie strode into the Turkish barbershop next to Daphne's. The shop buzzed with electric razors, the scent of shaving cream and too much aftershave heavy in the air. Occupied by men only, it must have been a while since a woman stepped foot inside, judging by their confused stares. She walked down the middle of the chairs to the familiar sight of Norman hunched over a slot machine at the far end of the shop.

Norman greeted her with his usual grumble. "You got me barred from Platts."

"That's not how I remember it, Norman," Jessie

replied, leaning against the machine. "And that doesn't sound like an apology to me."

"I am," Norman snapped.

"Are what?"

"Sorry," he said, feeding another coin to the machine. "Should never have put my hands on a woman like that."

"Or anyone," Jessie corrected, her tone stern. "But apology accepted."

There was a temptation to mention the secret Hilda had shared about his daughter, but she decided against it. That wasn't why she was there. Instead, she leaned in and whispered, "I know you're not as tough as you make yourself out to be, Norman. We know who killed Ronnie."

"So what?" Norman continued to jab the buttons.

"If you want to help, follow me."

Without waiting for his response, Jessie set off back through the shop. Outside, she spotted her dad deep in conversation with Benedict Langley as they walked across the courtyard. Jessie would have gambled her last pound coin that Benedict was bragging about his plans for Fern Moore. Barker noticed her and gave a small nod of acknowledgement.

The slot machine fell silent, and Norman followed her out, muttering under his breath. As she shut the door behind him, she let out a relieved breath.

"How's that lad doing, anyhow?" Norman asked, the rare compassion taking her by surprise. "The one who fell off the scooter?"

"Once he woke up from surgery, we couldn't shut him up. He'll be fine."

"Where we off to then?" Norman asked.

"You'll see."

"This better not be a stitch-up."

"Oh, it is," she said, winking at him. "Just not yours."

~

Clipped footsteps echoed outside the food bank, sending Julia's heart into a panicked rhythm. Hilda, standing by her side, looked stricken as the colour drained from her face. Audrey, back to flipping through the pages of the clipboard, seemed blissfully unaware.

"It's time for Ronnie to rest," Hilda whispered to Julia. "And Georgiana."

"I couldn't agree more."

The quiet tension shattered as Barker appeared in the doorway, leading Benedict inside the food bank.

His hair was oiled, his tie a greedy shade of green, and an oblivious smug grin split his face.

"Glad to hear you've reconsidered, Hilda," Benedict said, his hands spread wide "But hey, even the best of us get it wrong sometimes. Takes a classy lady to admit her mistakes, so I'm glad we can talk about my vision for this place."

"What's going on?" Audrey asked.

Her question went unanswered, hanging heavy in the silence. Moments later, Jessie and Norman entered. Jessie dragged the shutters down, prompting Hilda to jump.

"What is going on?" Audrey repeated, her voice trembling.

"We're here for a business meeting, Audrey," Benedict chuckled, his grin widening. "Relax."

"You're an idiot," Jessie said under her breath.

Benedict looked to Barker, as though for an explanation, but Barker retreated to stand beside Julia near the shelves, leaving Benedict stranded in the centre of the room. Audrey clutched a clipboard to her chest, her eyes darting around, pressed against the wall.

The stage was set, and Julia stepped forward with a clearing of her throat.

"So, Benedict," Julia said, forcing what little of a

smile she could. "Tell us about your plans. Turning the flats into short-term holiday lets?"

Benedict pulled up a chair and crossed one leg over the other, happy to entertain his audience if his arrogant smile was anything to go by.

"It's brilliant," Benedict said. "The flats around here are practically being given away."

Hilda snorted. "That's what happens when you undervalue people."

"Business *is* business."

Jessie leaned against the rattling shutters, and asked, "Where are you getting the money from? You went bankrupt down in Cornwall, right?"

"Investors," he replied, his tone curt. "How do you know about—"

"Why aren't you developing the flats?" Hilda pressed. "You've bought fourteen by my last count, and they're sitting empty."

"All part of the plan, I assure you," Benedict responded, a triumphant smirk tugging at his lips. "Keeps the property values low while I'm in the acquisition phase. There have been plenty of developers renovating flats, installing new windows and doors, and making the place look too nice too soon. It's driven the prices up twenty percent this year alone! So, I had to go even cheaper. I'm still paying people, and I still get to make a *real* difference in this place. Once I clear out more of the riffraff, I'll execute my vision. So, how many of you are looking to invest? It's the perfect time."

"Idiot," Audrey muttered under her breath during a slow blink.

Norman dove forward and Jessie kicked off the shutters, lunging to drag him back.

"*Riffraff?*" he bellowed. "Who are you calling riffraff?"

The room fell into silence again, as Benedict looked around, the penny still floating around in the air with no sign of dropping soon.

"Do you regret it, Audrey?" Julia's voice cut through the stillness like a blade. "Agreeing to poison Ronnie for him?"

Audrey's face lost all muscle tension at the question as silence closed in again. A pin drop would have echoed like a gunshot. As the meaning of Julia's words sank in, Benedict's smirk slipped from his lips.

The game was up, and he'd noticed.

Audrey attempted to laugh, looking to Hilda for support, but she was back to being unable to look at her.

Barker cleared his throat and stepped forward, and said, "Would you like to hear the timeline, Audrey?"

Audrey said nothing.

"I would," Norman said.

Barker nodded, then tossed Benedict his green diary. "You should be more cautious about where you leave this."

Benedict's jaw moved up and down, but no sound passed his lips.

"So, it seems this whole sordid affair kicked off about a fortnight ago," Barker began, his voice grave and official. "Ronnie overheard Hilda refusing to be a part of your little plan, Benedict. He was furious, protective as a bulldog over this estate. That would have been when he assaulted you, pinned you up against the wall. I can only imagine what he said to you, but it was enough to rattle you. Care to elaborate for us?"

Barker paused, arching an eyebrow in Benedict's direction. Instead of answering, Benedict ran his fingers through his hair and cast a desperate look towards the shutters. His escape route was blocked by Jessie and Norman.

"Undeterred by Ronnie's threats, demands, accusations, whatever it is was, you removed the obstacle," Barker said. "You hatched a plan to have Ronnie killed. And, to do your dirty work, you persuaded someone Ronnie trusted."

Barker paused, casting a sideways glance at Audrey. "Maybe you were always planning to do it this past weekend, or perhaps Benedict's cast-iron alibi was a fortunate coincidence. Well, fortunate for Benedict, for a short time. Either way, Audrey, it was *you* who administered the poison, wasn't it? The poison derived from the castor beans grown in Hilda's garden."

Audrey tried another dismissive laugh, but Norman raised a shaking finger, pointing right at her.

"I remember seeing *you* at lunch with Ronnie that day," Norman growled. "Ronnie was doing all the talking, and I didn't understand then. I thought he was planning to convert our dad's flat into a holiday home. I was furious. That's why I confronted him."

"He was telling you what you already knew," Julia said. "You'd been meeting with Benedict. Ronnie's *love bird*."

"After Ronnie broke into my home," Hilda said, looking up at Audrey with a dark gaze. "He went to see you. He must have thought you were going to help him. He had his proof against me, against Benedict, and he trusted *you*. You knew Georgiana always brought in something sweet from that bakery she liked, and Ronnie never said no to them."

"Why would *I* kill Ronnie?" Audrey pleaded, taking a step in Hilda's direction. "What reason would I have?"

Julia pulled the photograph out of her back pocket.

"You've been rather inconsistent about your relationship with Ronnie," Julia said. "First, you claimed you didn't really know him. School acquaintances. What was it you said? Are any of us the same people we were as teenagers?" She paused, watching Audrey squirm further into the wall. "Then, when I asked you again, knowing that you'd been crying on Hilda's sofa, you slipped up and admitted you once lived here. But there's a bit more to the story, isn't there?" She offered the picture to Audrey but she didn't look at it. "This picture was taken on February 5th 1986. That was the last day you saw Ronnie before he left for the army, wasn't it?"

"I don't know what you're talking about," she said, the denial coming out quieter than the previous times. "That's not me. You can't prove it."

"I asked DI Moyes to check his army records," Barker revealed, a detail even Julia didn't know. "His official enlistment date was February 6th 1986. It *was* the last day you saw him in Fern Moore."

"You confessed it yourself, Audrey," Julia pressed on. "Ronnie came back a changed man. You couldn't bear to be around him. You detested watching the man you once loved being a shadow of himself, all while hogging the limelight at the food bank you'd given so many years to. The food bank you were threatened and robbed at. Drained of your energy, pulled between here and your job. Resenting Georgiana for having all the time in the world, and hating Ronnie for making it all look so easy."

Audrey's mouth twisted, tears welling up in her eyes. She gritted her teeth, clenching her hands into fists. "He would destroy this place given enough time," she hissed. "Georgiana found out he was stealing food for donations. Ronnie was about to bring trouble down upon us all."

"Ronnie was *paying* for that food," Jessie said. "He was using his army pension to keep Fern Moore fed. You keep such diligent records here, Hilda was able to work out an average of how much food he was bringing in, and what it might cost wholesale. Give or take a few hundred, it's almost the exact amount missing from his secret savings. He was buying that stuff from the local cash and carry. Georgiana admitted to me she had no proof. She made it up because it sounded right to her, looking down on him from a great height."

"How *could* you, Audrey?" Hilda cried. "After *all* this time, how *could* you?"

"I was tired, Hilda," she said, letting the clipboard slip from her grip. "Tired of trying to save the world. Tired of having to keep fighting against the odds, everything getting harder every year. And the people around here. Don't you ever tire of the way they talk to us, the way they treat us, after everything we do for them? Benedict offered me a way out when he saw Ronnie talking to me, getting a little too close, trying a little too hard. If I did what Benedict asked, and cleared the path for him to do what he wanted at Fern Moore, he'd give me enough money so I could disappear from this place."

With everyone hanging on Audrey's every word, Benedict jumped up and seized Hilda. Wrapping an arm around her neck, he looked around, but there was nothing to use as a weapon.

"Let go of her," Barker demanded, approaching with open palms. "The game is up, Benedict. You've lost."

Growling like a caged dog, Benedict shoved Hilda across the room in Julia's direction. With a quick reflex, Julia caught her, but the momentum of the throw sent them crashing into the nearest shelf. Losing all sense of gravity, and the weight of Hilda on her, Julia fell back onto the shelf, unable to stop the domino effect. The food that they had spent all day organising, for Audrey to reorganise, came crashing down. Jars smashed, boxes burst open, and cans rolled in every direction.

Silence fell, and Julia allowed herself a sigh of

relief, but her relief vanished as soon as it arrived. Above them on the leaning shelves, a massive crate teetered on the edge. Jessie lunged forward, dragging Hilda off Julia. Julia rolled away, a hair's breadth from disaster. Bananas from the crate hit the floor in a mass, their ripe bodies squishing and bursting upon impact with the ground in a crash of broken wood.

Benedict, in his headlong rush to escape, found himself the victim of his own destruction. His foot landed on a banana peel, and with a yelp, he collided headfirst with the shutters. But he wasn't giving up. He gathered himself, shaking off the shock, and with a vengeful push, he shoved the front table towards Norman.

Benedict turned back to survey the havoc he'd wreaked, a smug grin stretching across his face.

"Sorry," he said, bending over, "but I think it's time I split."

But his satisfaction was short-lived. The shutters screeched upwards from the outside, and there stood DI Moyes, backed by six uniformed police officers. Their grins mirrored Benedict's, only growing wider as Benedict's faded.

"I didn't poison Georgiana," Audrey protested, wriggling free of the shelf that had pinned her to the wall. "I'm not going down for that one too. Benedict was at Wellington Heights for an apartment viewing.

He asked me for the ricin I made and he poisoned the macarons on the doorstep when he saw her name on the order."

"You're a *monster*," Jessie cried, and it was Norman's turn to hold Jessie back. "You killed your own stepsister?"

"Georgiana was too bored of her privileged life," he sneered, wrestling with the officers gripping him in place. "She had nothing else to do but volunteer her time and pay attention to what I was doing. For a dumb blonde, she put most of it together in the end. I can't believe she waited around that long thinking I was going to show up for that drink."

"At least she was trying to make a difference," Hilda shot back. "Unlike you."

PC Puglisi cuffed Audrey, and not without asking Barker how his book was coming along. When the two culprits were driven away, DI Moyes lingered with them outside of the food bank as they stared at the destruction while Hilda picked through the stock to salvage what she could.

"Thank Billy Matthews for that footage of Audrey moving Ronnie's body to his flat on Friday night in that shopping trolley," Moyes said, patting Jessie on the shoulder. "No wonder nobody came forward."

"She always did the deliveries," Julia remembered. "Nothing out of the ordinary."

"I hope he's on the mend," Moyes said, stepping back. "Good work everyone. I'll leave you to clean up the mess."

Joining Hilda, Julia pulled her away from the destruction and forced her into the chair Benedict had delivered his confession from.

"It's over," Julia said, as she stared at the pile of bananas that had almost landed on them. "And thanks to Ronnie, you'll be able to replace all of this in no time."

~

A wild street party broke out at Fern Moore once the police cleared off, but Jessie found herself at the hospital visiting Billy. She stayed outside his room for a while, watching Paige fluff up his pillows. When Paige noticed Jessie, she excused herself, and Jessie set the bouquet she'd bought from CostSavers on the bedside table. Sinking into the chair, she let the stress of the evening melt away. Seeing Billy upright in bed was a tonic.

"You're looking better."

"Won't be lifting weights anytime soon," he lifted the cast arm laid across his torso. "Fancy signing it?"

Their shared laughter filled the sterile room, but Billy's eyes soon dimmed.

"I still can't believe what happened to Ronnie," he said. "But at least the truth is out now."

"You were right about him," Jessie said. "In the end, he was more than a good guy. He was a great guy."

With a groan, Billy sat up a little. "Did you mean what you said about us being friends?"

Surprised, Jessie paused for a second before replying, "I'd want nothing more, Billy."

"Wasn't sure if it was just the alcohol talking."

"How about a McSizzle's chicken wrap and a can of beer on a bench next time for old time's sake?" she said with a wink. "What made you think to go back over the camera footage?"

"The trolley," he said. "I heard it from inside the flat right before Ronnie's TV was turned on. I didn't think anything of it until word got around about him being moved. We all got used to the sound of Audrey's deliveries, but never on a Friday night. Even the police looked past it. They had Paige's camera footage from day one."

"Billy Matthews saves the day."

"Maybe I'm not so useless after all."

Jessie shook her head. "You were never."

"Still unemployed, and this won't help," he said, nodding at the cast. "And it's not like I even know what I want to do."

"If you don't know what you want to do, just try to make a difference," she said. "Use that passion you had for protecting your community when you wanted to flatten Benedict and channel it into something good."

Billy looked thoughtful. "Yeah? Like what?"

"Hilda has big plans for the food bank now that she's got Ronnie's money," she told him. "I heard her talking to my mum before I left. She's planning to hire staff, so she's not relying on volunteers forever. She wants to make sure the food bank continues even after she's gone."

"You think I could?"

"You'd be perfect for it, Billy. You're a Fern Moore native, and deep down, you're a good guy, too."

"Am I?"

"Of course you are," Jessie reassured him. "Just promise me two things."

"Anything."

"No more using these when you're frustrated." She patted his hand poking out of the cast. "And if I ever see you on that scooter again, you'll have more than a broken arm."

"Deal."

Paige returned with a tray of three cups and passed them around.

"I heard about what happened tonight," Paige

said, stepping back, tucking her red hair behind her ears. "He didn't deserve what happened to him. Talking to Billy, he's helped me see it wasn't Ronnie's fault what happened to Josh. It was just bad luck. Hearing that Ronnie had been giving all his spare cash to help everyone out, some of the food would have ended up in my kitchen. He kept my girls fed. I'm thankful for that, even if his TV was too loud."

"To Ronnie," Billy said, lifting his cup in his working hard. "And his loud telly."

22

A month had passed since the scandalous revelations that had rocked Fern Moore, and on a cool August morning, a modest crowd had gathered for the unveiling of the Ronnie Roberts memorial bench in the heart of Fern Moore.

'For Ronnie - A true Fern Moore hero.'

Among the locals, Julia, Barker, and Olivia were sharing in the joy and sadness, as they enjoyed hot dogs from the food bank's BBQ, run by a freshly shaved Norman.

Standing before the crowd on a log in the central playpark, Hilda held herself tall, her voice ringing out over the murmuring onlookers. She spoke about never giving up, about the importance of helping the remaining residents of Fern Moore for as long as Ronnie's generosity lasted, and about the necessity of preventing any further schemes from people like Benedict Langley. She ended the speech by repeating her father's advice.

"If someone is brave enough to ask for help," she said, looking out at the crowd hanging on every word, "be brave enough to give it, if you can."

Hilda climbed down to applause and found Julia in the crowd.

"Great turnout," Julia said.

"Great hotdogs," Barker added.

"Hotdogs," Olivia repeated, sounding like 'hogdogs.'

"None of this would have been possible without Ronnie, and of course, you, Julia." Hilda bowed to her. "Your grandmother was right about you. You are quite the detective."

"Anyone could have figured it out."

"You're far too modest." Hilda's cheeks peaked from a smile, looking freer than she had in the month Julia had known her. "Thank your daughter for suggesting Billy. He's stepped up to the plate in a way I've never seen from him."

Looking around for Billy, she waved to him on the other side of the courtyard by a tree Julia had never noticed. Paige was there too with her girls.

"We planted a tree for Josh last night. Paige wanted something a little more lowkey, and after what I put her through when I was blind to Benedict's scheme, I was more than happy to oblige. And Norman has been a great help, too. He's turned out to be quite the volunteer."

"Peace in Fern Moore at last," Barker said, finishing his hot dog with a lick of his fingers. "Want another, Olivia?"

"No!"

"Are you sure?"

"No!"

"Are you just saying 'no' because it's your new favourite word?"

"No!"

Julia almost followed them as they walked towards Norman at the BBQ, but she sensed Hilda had more to share.

"Cup of tea," Hilda said. "On me."

After talking about all of Hilda's plans for the food bank and how she was going to put Ronnie's money to good use, fiddling with the sugar sachets the whole time, Julia pushed her for what was on her mind.

"I went to see Benedict," Hilda began, her voice thick with distaste. "He's put all the flats he bought up for sale with a pledge to sell only to first-time buyers. I don't know whether he's genuinely remorseful or just looking for a way to spite his investor, but it's a start."

"No holiday flats then?"

"Not at Fern Moore," Hilda said, looking through the window with a smile. "Silly idea, really. You can paint over the graffiti as much as you want, it's never going to be the hottest holiday destination, Cotswolds or not."

"And Audrey?"

Hilda's smile dropped.

"She requested I go to see her," she said, dropping the sugar. "I declined. After all our years working together, I didn't notice how much her poor attitude was poisoning mine." She paused, possibly at her choice of words, and said, "We still don't know where Ronnie died..." Hilda's voice vanished, but she composed herself. "I imagine when he realised he was ill, he sought someone he thought he could trust. He didn't come to me, and that will be a forever regret of mine. Wherever he died, Audrey transported his body with that trolley to his flat to make it look like he'd died in his chair watching his favourite programme. She confessed in her letter to me she guessed the combination on the first attempt based on that date. The paperwork he took from me was in there, and she destroyed it on Benedict's behalf. I will never forgive her for how she betrayed Ronnie."

With that, Hilda stood, glancing out of the window as a white van pulled up outside. "Ah, they're here. I set some money aside from the sale of Ronnie's flat to replace the lift. We can help the community in more ways than one now, and frankly, I'm tired of those stairs."

"You and me both," Julia said, remembering having dragged the trolley up. Her imagination filled in the image of Audrey doing the same on that fateful night, but she shook it away. "You're going to do great things here, Hilda."

"Wouldn't be here without you. I'll never forget that." Hilda was almost out of the door when she turned back, her expression grave. "Benedict revealed who his investor was to me," she said. "It was James Jacobson."

Julia froze, the name turning her stomach.

"I know you and Barker helped him during the library debacle," she said, "I want you to be careful. I spoke to some old friends at the council. Just ... be careful."

"I haven't seen him in over a year."

Hilda offered a tight smile, thanked Julia one more time for everything she'd done, and then walked out of the café, leaving Julia wondering what the warning could mean.

The antique desk creaked under Jessie's grip as she manoeuvred it through the door of *The Peridale Post*'s new office above Katie's salon. Veronica followed right behind, the tantalising aroma of fish and chips wafting from a bag in her hands.

Veronica paused as she landed on the unopened envelope sitting on Jessie's desk. "Are these your exam results? Why haven't you opened them yet?"

"What if I failed?"

"What if you did?" Veronica ripped open the envelope, an impish grin on her face. "You still need to know."

Jessie scanned the page, a slow smile spreading across her face. "C in Science and Maths. A in English."

"See!" Veronica clapped her on the back. "That's fantastic! An A where it counts. Now, time to do what most people do after their exams and forget everything you learned. We have a mountain of *actual work* to do in this office."

"Remember, I'm still part-time. I have—"

"The café, I know." Veronica cut her off with a wave of her hand. "Just take the stories you're interested in, that's all I want from you. I'll send the others out to do the grunt work. I'll make an investigative journalist of you yet if it kills me."

Sensing it was the right moment, Jessie reached into the desk's drawer, pulling out a present wrapped in bright pink paper. "A retirement gift, since you're finished at the college too. I know you didn't want a fuss, but you said it was your favourite, and..."

Veronica unwrapped the paper to reveal the first edition of *To Kill a Mockingbird* that Julia's dad had helped her track down. Jessie hadn't expected tears, but that's what she got.

"I know you're ready to move on from it," Jessie said with a shrug, "but if I've learned anything this past month, it's that you don't have to leave your past behind every time you want to move forward. You can still take a little piece with you."

"Oh, you sentimental scoundrel," Veronica said, batting the tears from underneath her pink glasses. "Jessie, this is perfect. I've been teaching this book for thirty years. Thank you."

Katie interrupted their tender moment, charging in and popping a bottle of champagne between them, inches from both of their faces.

"This is going to be so much fun!" She rested three champagne flutes on the desk and poured them generous amounts before passing them around. "What are we toasting to?"

"New beginnings?" Veronica suggested.

"That didn't go too well last time," Jessie said. "What the heck. To new beginnings."

After their toast, Katie's gaze fell on the antique desk.

"Look at that. Still standing strong, I see." Katie gave it a jovial kick, and one leg collapsed, crashing the desk to the floor. Turning, she ran down the stairs, crying, "*Brian*! What did I tell you about that desk?"

Staring at her broken desk, Jessie could only laugh.

"She'll take some getting used to," Veronica whispered. "So, straight to business, then?"

"So soon?"

"No time like the present." Veronica cracked open a laptop on her desk on the other side of the room, and said, "Johnny's old council informant has just reactivated and started sending things to the paper, which is never a good sign. It seems Greg Morgan, our local MP, had a hand in Fern Moore's 'clearing out'. No doubt he wanted to claim he'd 'cleaned up the area.'"

"And he didn't succeed."

"Not this time," Veronica glanced up at her, her face serious. "I'm counting down the days until I have something concrete that I can blast across the front page, but right now, he's still too slippery for his own good. But he *will* slip up."

"You really don't like him, do you?" Jessie asked, perching on the edge of Veronica's sturdier desk. "Is he an ex, or something?"

"Or something." Veronica closed the laptop. "So, what about your ex? How'd that all end up for you?"

"Nice try. What aren't you telling me?"

"*Tons*," Veronica said, raising her glass with a wink. "Here's to the next storm."

~

In the quiet hush of an early August afternoon, Julia's Café was far from its usual Saturday frenzy, but a comforting peace had taken its place. The early summer heat had tempered, replaced by much cooler weather. Behind the counter, Sue, Julia, and Jessie shared the space, savouring the rare quietness.

"Just goes to show. We shouldn't wish for things to stay the same," Julia said, reading over Jessie's exam results. "You'd never have gone to college if nothing ever changed. I'm so proud of you, Jessie. This, your new job at the paper, everything."

"We *all* are," Sue said. "We'll have to go across to the bar to celebrate later."

The trio behind the counter glanced up as the door to the café swung open with a creak. Dot shuffled in with her cart, leaving Percy and the dogs to lap the green. She went straight to the corner where donations for the food bank were stacked in a basket and began to transfer them with Olivia's help, who'd been happily ambling around the café saying her new favourite word to every request.

Soon after Evelyn, resplendent in a turquoise ensemble, glided in. She made her way towards her usual table and ordered her tea. All the while, Barker was stationed in the corner, his fingers dancing over the keys of his laptop, lost in the world of his latest manuscript. The day was as regular as they came in Peridale. A gentle reminder of the rhythm of life in the quaint village, that, despite occasional interruptions, was a comforting constant.

"I can't believe it!" Barker announced, staring up from his laptop with wide-eyed disbelief. "I just finished the first draft."

"Are you trying to outdo me?" Jessie asked, shaking her exam results. "But congrats, Dad. When's it coming out? Are you going down the publishing company route again?"

"After last time, I'm not sure, but I had a somewhat interesting email land in my inbox this morning." He reached around them for the last slice of what Julia had promised would be her last batch of banana bread for a while; the smell was turning against her. "An indie film crew wants to make a documentary about me."

"A *film* crew?" Dot popped up out of the food basket as she transferred the donations to her cart. "Why would they want to make a documentary about you?"

"Dad had a bestselling book, don't forget," Jessie pointed out. "But yeah, what for?"

"And soon to have a second," Julia assured him. "What did you say to them?"

"Still deciding, but from the sounds of it, they're interested in the whole DI to author to PI angle." Barker dusted the crumbs from his hands. "I'll sleep on it."

"I foresee it being a great success," Evelyn said, swirling her cup. "The book *and* the documentary."

Sighing, Barker said, "Now why did she have to say that?" Distracted by a van pulling up outside, he walked around the counter, and said, "That'll be my new client chair. Is everyone sure they don't know what happened to the old one? It vanished into thin air."

"It's a real mystery," Jessie said, slipping through the beaded curtain into the kitchen.

When Barker was outside directing the delivery

driver down the alley with the large cardboard box, Dot glanced up from the donations box, where Olivia had joined the help with the transfer.

"Quite the great heist, by the sounds of it. Not the brightest PI around if he can't locate one simple office chair," Dot said with a purse of her lips. In a lower voice, she said, "I saw you and Jessie dragging that thing into her flat last month, Julia."

"That's because you spend far too much time at the window, Gran," Sue said.

"I predict Barker knows where the chair is," Evelyn announced, "and he's more than happy to let it go."

"We'll see," Jessie said, popping her head back through the beads. "Who's volunteering to help me drag it to Mulberry Lane? Gonna need a new desk while I'm at it, too. Do you think he'll notice if I take his?"

"I predict so."

"And *I* predict," Dot called, as she tossed the last tin into the cart, "that you'll stop predicting things any second now."

"Evelyn's actually quite spot-on," Sue said, wiping down the front of the display cabinet after Olivia pressed her entire face up against the glass. "Her horoscopes are always accurate to me. And remember the skull in the tea leaves?"

Evelyn frowned. "Skull?"

"The morning Dot came in with the newspaper about Ronnie," Julia reminded her. "You saw a skull and rushed back to the B&B."

"Oh no, dear, *I* didn't see a skull," Evelyn said with a hearty chuckle. "I saw the most detailed image of my B&B engulfed in flames. I rushed back home to find one of my guests burning toast." She sipped her tea and peered into the cup. "Today, I see a beautiful shining sun. A lovely, clear day, perfect for bathing in tonight's full moon."

"Julia, my dear," Dot said, on her way to the door with the week's donations for the food bank. "Whatever you're putting in Evelyn's tea, count me out!"

But the universe did indeed work in mysterious ways, and at that very moment, clouds rolled in, and soft rain pattered against the café's window. Julia laughed, glad things were, indeed, very much back to normal.

Thank you for reading, and don't forget to
RATE/REVIEW!

The Peridale Cafe story continues in...

ETON MESS AND ENEMIES
Coming soon!

Sign up to Agatha Frost's newsletter to be the first to hear about its release!

Thank you for reading!

DON'T FORGET TO RATE AND REVIEW ON AMAZON

Reviews are more important than ever, so show your support for the series by rating and reviewing the book on Amazon! Reviews are **CRUCIAL** for the longevity of any series, and they're the best way to let authors know you want more! They help us reach more people! I appreciate any feedback, no matter how long or short. It's a great way of letting other cozy mystery fans know what you thought about the book.

Being an independent author means this is my livelihood, and *every review* really does make a **huge difference.** Reviews are the best way to support me so I can continue doing what I love, which is bringing you, the readers, more fun cozy adventures!

WANT TO BE KEPT UP TO DATE WITH AGATHA FROST RELEASES? *SIGN UP THE FREE NEWSLETTER!*

www.AgathaFrost.com

You can also follow **Agatha Frost** across social media. Search 'Agatha Frost' on:

Facebook
Twitter
Goodreads
Instagram

ALSO BY AGATHA FROST

Claire's Candles
1. Vanilla Bean Vengeance
2. Black Cherry Betrayal
3. Coconut Milk Casualty
4. Rose Petal Revenge
5. Fresh Linen Fraud
6. Toffee Apple Torment
7. Candy Cane Conspiracies

Peridale Cafe
1. Pancakes and Corpses
2. Lemonade and Lies
3. Doughnuts and Deception
4. Chocolate Cake and Chaos
5. Shortbread and Sorrow
6. Espresso and Evil
7. Macarons and Mayhem
8. Fruit Cake and Fear
9. Birthday Cake and Bodies
10. Gingerbread and Ghosts

11. Cupcakes and Casualties
12. Blueberry Muffins and Misfortune
13. Ice Cream and Incidents
14. Champagne and Catastrophes
15. Wedding Cake and Woes
16. Red Velvet and Revenge
17. Vegetables and Vengeance
18. Cheesecake and Confusion
19. Brownies and Bloodshed
20. Cocktails and Cowardice
21. Profiteroles and Poison
22. Scones and Scandal
23. Raspberry Lemonade and Ruin
24. Popcorn and Panic
25. Marshmallows and Memories
26. Carrot Cake and Concern
27. Banana Bread and Betrayal

Other

The Agatha Frost Winter Anthology

Peridale Cafe Book 1-10

Peridale Cafe Book 11-20

Claire's Candles Book 1-3

Printed in Great Britain
by Amazon